Faith Sloan

Knot Your Average Love Story

Primal Surrender

Cypress City Seductions Series

Also by Faith Sloan

The Busy Witch: A Guide for Modern Witches
An Ember of Darkness: Beyond the Veil Chronicles
(book one) Audiobook release October 31, 2025
An Ember of Ruin: Beyond the Veil Chronicles (book
two) Coming 2025
Depths of Desire: Cypress City Seductions (book two)
Audiobook 2026

To the good little rope bunnies,
and the hungry wolves.

Come out,
Come out,
Wherever you are.

Chapter One

The Devil's Contract

Squinting against the glare of a techno-colored strobe light, I blocked the beam with my hand as I shouldered my way through a throng of sweaty, gyrating bodies. The fog machine made it difficult to spot the woman I was here to see. Difficult, but not impossible. Her hot pink bandage dress glowed under the black light, honing in my sight like a beacon.

Bass thundered through the floorboards and up through my bones, each beat matching the throb of tension in my temples. The crowd pressed in from all sides—designer perfumes mixing with spilled drinks and desperation. A guy in a mesh tank top stumbled into me, his pupils blown wide, mumbling an apology I couldn't hear over the relentless EDM.

I kept my eyes locked on that dress, watching it weave through the chaos like a shark fin through choppy waters. She hadn't spotted me yet. The temperature spiked ten degrees as I closed in. Neon-painted dancers on elevated platforms cast writhing shadows across her face, but I could still make out that signature red lipstick smile. She turned, a glass of champagne dangling from manicured fingers, and I saw the exact moment recognition flickered in those cat-like eyes.

"Alex, to what do I owe the pleasure?" She purred, slinking closer and gently tapping my face, causing her bejeweled bangles to jingle. Her voice carried a hypnotic undertone, the kind that made promises feel like silk across skin—promises that would slowly strangle you if you weren't careful.

"I'm here to resolve our contract." I tried to keep my voice steady. The money I'd been saving since before running away was in the duffle bag hanging over my shoulder. I was finally going to be free of her and this club forever.

Her smile widened, revealing teeth too sharp to be human. The surrounding air shimmered like heat waves off hot asphalt.

The Madam laughed, "Oh, Alex. You still owe me quite a bit for breaking our contract early. With interest, it's grown to...what was it now? Fifty thousand?"

My mouth went dry. Of course she'd try to change the deal last minute. "That wasn't our agreement. The buyout was five thousand."

She leaned in close, her breath smelling of expensive wine and ozone. "Times are tough without my Will-o'-Wisp. If you come back to Ogygia, you can work it off on time."

"Get bent, Michelle. There's no way I'm coming back to work for you." She *hmphed* and jerked her head towards the door. Two hulking shapes materialized from the shadows. The Madam's enforcers: one with skin like granite, the other wreathed in perpetual darkness. Their hands clamped down on my shoulders with inhuman strength.

"Now darlin'," the Madam said, examining her nails, "about my money…"

"I don't have fifty thousand and you know it. I *have* what we agreed on, right here in this bag."

The bruiser's fist connected with my stomach. I doubled over, wheezing.

"I'm sure that your new boss at that drab little store could loan the rest to you." She said, leaning back against the bar. "Or, you could come crawling back to me. I'd make sure you're taken care of." The patrons scooted away. They all knew who was boss here, and it wasn't me.

The smokey one grabbed my collar and started dragging me toward the back exit. One of his tendrils snatched the duffle bag off my shoulder and placed it at the Madam's feet. The crowd parted like water, their eyes glazed over—the club's glamour made them ignore the violence.

"Think about my offer, Alex!" The Madam called after me. "I'm always hiring." They threw me into the alley hard enough to scrape my palms on the concrete. The door slammed shut, leaving me alone with the distant thump of bass and the taste of copper in my mouth.

The gravel dug deeper into the jagged scrapes in my calloused hands as I pushed myself up off the pavement. Bracing against the grime laden brick wall, I pulled myself to my feet. Each breath was a struggle as I tried to suck down the panic mounting in my chest. The world blurred around the edges, but the pain in my hands kept me grounded.

Ogygia was a nightclub for the creatures of the night to flaunt their talents and lure lusty human patrons into emptying their pockets. I'd worked here as a barten der...and later as an escort. When Madam Michelle realized how easily the mortals fell for my charms, she'd perfected the art of seduction into a predatory science—selling illusions as addictive as any drug, promising dreams that would consume those who believed in them.

She sold me to whomever would pay the most for an hour in a curtained corner. In those secluded areas, which should have been private, she'd hidden cameras. Anyone in the world could watch what I did with those high paying clients, for a fee. A fee, mind you, that I never saw a dime of.

The neon sign above cast a sickly green glow across the wet asphalt. Music still pulsed through the walls, but out here it sounded hollow, like a heartbeat echoing through an empty chest. A rat scurried past, its eyes gleaming an unnatural violet—one of the Madam's many spies, no doubt. Even the vermin in this part of town answered to her.

Twyla's shop felt worlds away now. I'd built that life from scratch after escaping this place—the honest work of crafting belts, wallets, and armor–the simple pride of creating something with my own hands. My calluses were earned through that redemption, not through serving the whims of monsters who wore designer suits and diamond rings.

They all wanted my 'gift', that damned ancestral charm that made mortals want to please us, protect us, give us anything we asked for. I'd tried to suppress it. Madam Michelle had gotten to me though, whispering promises of power and wealth, of controlling the gift instead of hiding it. I'd ended up dancing on that cursed stage while creatures with teeth like needles and eyes like frozen stars watched from the VIP section. *¡Ay, carajo! This is never going to end.*

I became the star of her show—her 'Will-o'-Wisp', drawing patrons like moths to flame. My soft, almost feminine features combined with my glamour magic made me irresistible. People would spend fortunes just to see me dance, crowding the stage with tips every night. But the real money came from the backrooms. High-class businessmen and women would pay obscene amounts for 'private dances'—a poorly disguised code for sex. What the Madam discovered, and what made her grip on me so tight, was that my glamour created a kind of addiction in humans.

The wealthy elite who sampled my talents once would inevitably return, spending more each time, investing in the club just to ensure their continued access to me. I was her golden goose, her perfect trap for the rich and powerful. As the money poured in, I realized with growing dread that she would never let me go. Even when my seven-year contract expired, she'd find some way to extend it—a clause I'd missed, a debt I couldn't repay, perhaps even outright blackmail with the recordings. When I finally understood the depth of my slavery—that she'd secretly filmed these encounters and sold the recordings worldwide—I knew I had to leave, contract be damned.

The back door creaked open, spilling out electronic bass and sweetened smoke. A couple stumbled into the alley—the woman's guise glamour flickering to reveal scaled skin beneath her sequined dress, her companion too enthralled to notice. They were too wrapped up in each other to see me, but I pressed deeper into the shadows, anyway. Old habits die hard in a place like this.

I pushed off from the wall, testing my legs. They held, barely. I needed a plan. There were others who'd escaped the Madam's clutches, others who owed her money or blood or years of their lives. *Maybe together we could...* The thought died as I spotted another rat watching me from behind a dumpster, unblinking. *No, I couldn't afford to think like that. Not here.* First, I needed to get somewhere safe, somewhere to lick my wounds.

The distant wail of sirens echoed off the buildings—another "accident" at one of the Madam's other establishments. This city belonged to her kind after dark, and the human authorities knew better than to look too closely. I limped toward the street, leaving bloody handprints on the wall that would be gone by morning.

Nothing in this alley lasted long enough to tell tales. If I didn't get a handle on this debt, neither would I.

Chapter Two

PREY

It was too early to go home. Twyla would be hip deep in whatever new project she'd started, and I didn't want to worry her with how I looked. My hair was still plastered to my skin from the heat of the club, and the biting night air sent goosebumps down my back in stark contrast.

The thought of climbing the creaky stairs to my apartment above the general store made my stomach twist. Twyla would be up there surrounded by half-finished craft projects, her purple micro braids catching the light as she bounced between them with her endless energy. She'd notice the blood, the bruises, the way I was favoring my left side. Twyla would see right through any excuse I made. She'd already taken a chance on me, giving me both a job and a home when my history should have sent her running. I couldn't burden her with this, too.

The street was dark as I headed to the bar, street lights flickering. With a quick glance to ensure no one was watching, I let a small orb of blue light form above my palm, just enough to illuminate the uneven sidewalk ahead. The familiar cool tingle of my magic was comforting after the day I'd had.

Instead, I ended up at The Rusty Nail, a dive bar just a few blocks from home. The familiar smell of stale beer and pretzels wrapped around me like an old blanket. A group of regulars clustered around the TV mounted above the bar, their collective groan at a fumbled play drowned out the classic rock playing over the speakers. No glamours here, no hidden cameras or supernatural predators lurking in dark corners. Just humans being human.

I slid onto the least sticky barstool and ordered a Dark 'n' Stormy. *"Carajo,"* I muttered under my breath, "what a fucking day." I rolled up my sleeves to keep them from sticking to the tacky bar surface, revealing the intricate tattoos that covered both arms from wrist to shoulder. The swirling designs—part tribal, part art nouveau—had been my one significant expense after escaping the Madam's world. Each session had felt like reclaiming another piece of myself, covering the skin she'd once treated as merchandise with art of my own choosing. I traced one of the spiraling patterns, following it as it wound around my forearm like smoke.

My phone buzzed—Madam Michelle, of course. A winky face and a heart, as if we were old friends sharing an inside joke. I could block her number, change my own, disappear into the city's sprawl. But…I just couldn't do it. So I did what I always did—ignored the message and scrolled social media instead, scrolling through pictures of other people's carefully curated lives.

The clock in the corner of my screen reminded me that Twyla would be up for hours yet reorganizing the store's entire inventory or designing new window displays with whatever craft supplies had caught her eye this week. The woman was a marketing genius when she could focus long enough to finish a project.

"This seat taken?" The voice rumbled like distant thunder. I looked up to find a mountain of a man indicating the empty stool beside me. Red hair and beard, both slightly wild, framed a face made for friendly smiles despite the impressive muscles that stretched his henley. *Damn.*

I shook my head, trying not to wince at the movement. "All yours."

"Rough night?" The redhead asked, gesturing to my scraped hands with his beer bottle. He spoke with an accent I couldn't quite place—something old world, but smoothed by years of American living.

"Something like that." I took another sip of my lime tinged drink, the burn helping to ground me.

He nodded, not pushing for details. "Kronos," he offered instead, extending a hand. I hesitated before taking it, surprised that his grip was gentle despite his size.

"Alex." The thrum of my magic caused his pupils to dilate. Guilt twisted in my stomach—I wasn't even trying to use it tonight, but sometimes it leaked out when I was tired or hurt. *Shit.* I slid my hand out of his, trying to put some distance between us. I wasn't in the mood for company. Especially not the obsessive kind my 'talents' enthralled.

"Greek?" I asked, trying to place his name. My knowledge of mythology was rusty at best, colored by what little I'd picked up from Twyla's info dump stories during slow days at the store. She'd had a fixation on mythos once she realized monsters were in fact real after the Great Revelation about ten years ago. That's how I got the job, telling her about my abilities. She didn't want to use them, though I would have to draw in clientele. No, she just wanted to ask about a million questions a day.

A smile played at the corners of his mouth. "Something like that."

The game ended, the crowd dispersed with good-natured arguing about bad calls and missed plays. The space between us felt charged and a little too intimate for my liking. Kronos ordered another round for both of us, sliding a fresh drink my way. I caught the lime before it could slip off the rim, my fingers brushing his. The contact sent electricity racing up my arm.

Kronos traced patterns in the condensation on his glass—strong, scarred hands that had seen their share of action. *I wonder what they'd look like wrapped around my throat.*

"You military?" I asked, noting the proud way he carried himself.

"Private sector." He took a slow sip of his drink.

"So what kind of private sector work are we talkin'?"

He took a slow sip of his beer, eyes never leaving mine. "I find people who don't want to be found."

The words should have set off warning bells, made me pull back. Instead, I shifted closer, intrigued. "That sounds like it could be a dangerous line of work."

"You could say that." His voice dropped lower, a rumble that I could feel in my chest. "Though I get the feeling you know something about dangerous work yourself."

"Nothing as exciting as hunting people down." I turned toward him fully now, my knee pressing against his thigh. His body radiated heat like a furnace. "Must make you a lot of friends."

"I've never had any complaints." There was something in his smile that made my pulse spike. His silver eyes glowed in the dim light of the bar. "When I want something, I tend to get it."

The rum made me bold. Or maybe it was the need to feel something–anything–other than the helplessness that had been choking me all night. I let my hand rest on his thigh, feeling the muscle tense under my touch. "And what do you want right now?"

His hand covered mine, thumb brushing over my knuckles. The touch was gentle, but there was restrained power in every movement. "I think you know what I want."

I drew in a shaky breath, hyper aware of every point of contact between us. "Oh yeah? Why don't you show me?"

Kronos's fingers tightened over mine, just enough pressure to make his strength clear. "Here?"

The word held weight, promise. I glanced around the bar—empty now except for the bartender wiping down tables and a couple arguing in the corner. "Your place nearby?"

"Just a few minutes" His other hand came to rest at the small of my back as we both stood, and I had to suppress a shiver at how easily it spanned the width of my spine. "Walking distance."

I tossed back the rest of my drink, letting the spice of the ginger beer burn down my throat. "Lead the way."

The frigid night air hit us as we stepped outside, making me crave the heat of his touch again. Before I could mourn the loss, he materialized at my side, his body deliberately close—our shoulders brushing, the back of his hand grazing mine with each step.

"Cold?" he asked, noticing my shiver. He shrugged out of his jacket and draped it over my shoulders. The scent of cedar mingled with the comforting warmth of the leather. I admired the obvious care Kronos took in his coat. *I bet he could take care of me just as well.*

"Thanks." I pulled it tighter around me, watching him from the corner of my eye. His stride was purposeful, predatory—a wolf on the prowl.

We passed under a streetlight, and for a moment his shadow seemed too large, too sharp. That had to be the drink playing tricks on me.

His hand caught my waist, pulling me into the shadow of a building. "Shortcut," he murmured, his breath hot against my ear. "Unless you've changed your mind?"

I turned in his grip, letting my back press against the rough brick. "Not a chance." I caught the front of his shirt, pulling him close. "If this is how you catch your bounties, I have some ethical concerns about your success rate."

His laugh was low, dangerous. "Depends on what I'm hunting." His hands settled on the wall on either side of my head, caging me in. "Is it working?"

The brick scraped against my back through his jacket as I arched closer. "You haven't caught me yet."

His fingers threaded through my hair, gentle until they weren't, pulling my head back to expose my throat. My breath hitched. "Haven't I?" His lips brushed my neck. Not quite a kiss, just the ghost of contact that made my skin prickle.

"I could slip away any time." I hooked my fingers through his belt loops, pulling his hips against mine.

"Could you?" His free hand slid down my side, finding the bruises from earlier. I couldn't quite hide my wince. He loosened his grip on my hair, concern flickering across his face. "You're hurt."

"I'm fine." I pulled him back when he withdrew, not ready to lose the heat of him. He studied me for a long moment.

Then he smiled—a sharp, hungry expression that made my pulse jump. "My place has a first aid kit. Among other things."

"Is that your professional pickup line?"

"Is it working?" His thumb traced my bottom lip, and I had to resist the urge to bite it.

"Depends on how close we are to testing it out." I let my teeth graze his finger anyway, watching his pupils dilate. "Because this alley, while exciting, isn't—"

He cut me off with a kiss that was nothing like the gentle touches from before. This was possession, claiming, a preview of what I was in for. His hands gripped my hips, pinning me to the wall as his tongue swept into my mouth. I tasted dark spices and something metallic, like the pressure before a storm.

When he pulled back, I was breathless and trying to hide my fluster. "Two more blocks," he growled against my lips. "Think you can behave that long?"

"Where's the fun in that?" I said, grabbing a fistful of his close cropped copper hair and sealing his lips with mine. I traced down his chest, undoing buttons as I went, until I could pull his shirt free.

"What happened to behaving?" His voice was rough with amusement, but he made no move to stop me. Kronos' appreciative murmurs encouraged me as I freed the fabric from his smooth torso, revealing the devastating cut of muscle trailing from his hips. My mouth watered at the sight, drawing me in to trail my lips over his exposed skin, nipping and teasing with my tongue as I sank to my knees. I ran my hand over him through his jeans, savoring his sharp intake of breath as he rocked back, fingers tightening in my hair. When he reached for his belt, I pushed his hands away. Meeting his darkened gaze, I pinched the zipper between my teeth and slowly pulled it down.

His cock sprung free of its restraints, nearly poking me in the eye. I had to lean back to take in the length of it. Thick, pulsing, and already dripping with pre-cum in anticipation. I balked. My mouth watered at the sight, imagining how it would feel sliding across my tongue.

The first taste of him flooded my senses—salt and heat and a faint pulse of…candy apples? I moaned at the weight of him on my tongue, at how perfectly he stretched my lips. My fingers dug into his thighs as I took him deeper, savoring how he throbbed against the roof of my mouth. His fingers threaded through my hair, calluses scraping deliciously against my scalp, making me shiver. When I hollowed my cheeks and swallowed around him, his sharp intake of breath rang like victory. I looked up through my lashes to watch his face, and the sight of his wanton carnal hunger made me ache with my own.

"Beautiful," he murmured, that strange accent thick with desire. His voice rumbled through me like thunder, making my skin prickle with heat. I swirled my tongue around him, showing off every trick I knew, reveling in the way his muscles tensed under my free hand. His fingers tightened in my hair—not pulling, just…there, a constant pressure encouraged me to keep going.

When I tried to speed up, to take control, his hands adjusted my movements. The change was so natural I didn't even notice at first, too caught up in the way his thighs trembled under my palms. Each growl vibrated through his body and into mine.

I looked up, drunk on the power I thought I had, only to find his silver eyes blazing with something ancient and wild. His thumb traced over my cheek with surprising tenderness, catching the corner of my lips. "That's it," he said, his voice like gravel and sin. The praise hit me like lightning, turning my bones to Jell-O.

Something shifted then—my calculated performance melting into pure instinct. My world narrowed to the taste of his skin, the way his hands guided me exactly where he wanted.

His cum flooded my mouth, hot and thick. I swallowed instinctively, heat coursing through me at his growl of approval. The sound of his zipper and belt buckle seemed loud in the sudden quiet as he tucked himself away. "Good boy," he breathed, fingers stroking my jaw as I finished swallowing. His hands were gentle as he pulled me to my feet, but before I could say anything clever, his mouth claimed mine. The kiss was devastating—deep and possessive, tasting himself on my tongue. My knees went weak, head spinning like I was the one who'd just found release.

When he broke the kiss, I could barely remember my name.

"You took me so well," Kronos murmured, his voice a low rumble as he stroked my cheek. "I'm going to take care of you just like that when we get to my apartment. It's just around the corner..." His silver eyes gleamed with promise.

Something twisted in my chest at his words, a strange plummeting sensation like my heart had dropped into my stomach. My mouth filled with the taste of copper, and I couldn't breathe. The alley seemed to narrow, the brick walls closing in.

His hand reached for mine, but I jerked back. "I can't—" The words stuck in my throat. "I can't do this."

Confusion crossed his features. "Alex?"

I shrugged off his jacket, thrusting it against his chest. "I'm sorry, I just—I can't."

But I was already backing away, my legs moving of their own accord. I turned and bolted down the alley, the night air biting against my skin without the borrowed warmth.

"Alex!" Kronos called after me, his voice echoing off the buildings. "Wait!"

I didn't look back, just kept running, each footfall sending jolts of pain through my already battered body. I didn't understand why I was running, why praise that should have felt good instead felt like hands around my throat. All I knew was that I needed to get away, needed air, needed space.

The familiar path home appeared before me. Three blocks. I just needed to make it three blocks. My lungs burned, but I pushed forward, past the closed bookstore, past the 24-hour laundromat with its harsh fluorescent glow, past the corner market where Twyla bought her favorite tea.

By the time I reached the general store, my side was screaming in pain and sweat had soaked through my shirt despite the cold. I paused at the door to the side entrance, listening for any sign of pursuit. Nothing but the distant sounds of the city at night. Fumbling with my keys, I slipped inside and began the long climb up the creaky stairs to the apartment.

Chapter Three

LEASHED

I lined up my tools with shaking hands: awl, needles, thread, rivets, all in their designated spots on the workbench. The routine of it settled something in my chest that had been fluttering since dawn, a meditation in metal and leather. Here, in my workspace, everything had its place. Everything made sense. The chaos of the world—of last night—couldn't touch me here.

I reached for my tooling knife, but paused when I noticed an intricate pattern I needed to trace. With practiced ease, I extended my index finger, a tiny blue flame blooming from the tip like a miniature torch. The cool fire cast perfect shadows on the leather, making the pattern easier to follow. This small use of my abilities had become second nature in my craft, though I'd never admit to Twyla how much it improved my work.

My fingers traced the familiar patterns worn into my wooden workbench, remembering how many hours

it had taken to arrange everything just so. Leather working had started as therapy. Something tactile to ground
me after escaping the Madam's world. Something honest.
Real. My reflection caught in the polished surface of a
brass rivet—blue eyes stark against dark tan skin, black
hair falling in my face again despite my best efforts to
tame it this morning.

I pushed my sleeves up, the tattooed designs on my
arms catching the morning light. The intricate patterns
had cost me months of savings, but they were worth
every penny—a permanent reminder that my body belonged to me now, not to the Madam or her clients.
Some customers at the shop would eye the tattoos, as if
the swirling designs marked me as dangerous or unpre-
dictable. Others, like Twyla, saw them as art. I wondered
what Kronos thought of them.

I'd barely made it home before sunrise, slipping
through the back entrance like a ghost. A hot shower
had washed away the evidence of the night, though
the phantom sensation of the length of Kronos in my
throat and hands still lingered on my skin. I'd managed
to get my clothes into the wash before Twyla's ear-
ly-morning energy could manifest. Not that she would
have judged—she wasn't the type—but her worry was its
own kind of weight. She'd taken enough chances on me
already, given me a job when my resume had more holes
than substance, offered me the apartment upstairs when
I'd been sleeping in my car. I didn't need her worrying
about me getting roughed up by my old life.

The front window of the store stopped me in my tracks, my reflection a dark shadow against her winter fantasy. Somehow, in the chaos of her late-night creative frenzy, Twyla had transformed it into a wonderland. Paper snowflakes danced on invisible threads, catching the morning light and casting prismatic patterns across my face. Crystalline branches, made from who-knows-what recycled materials. Knowing Twyla, probably salvaged from three different dumpster-diving expeditions—created an abstract forest scene. The mess she'd left behind—window paint in every shade of blue and white imaginable scattered across the bench, brushes soaking in cups of water, glitter absolutely everywhere—had taken an hour to clean up. But the result? A winter wonderland.

The counter bore faint smudges of paint where she couldn't decide between Arctic Blast and Midnight Frost for the snowdrift shadows. I'd found her notes scattered everywhere, covered in her signature purple gel ink: "More sparkle?" and "Check Pinterest for ice crystal references" and "Ask Alex about leather snowflakes???" Her handwriting as chaotic as her mind, ideas spilling across every available surface.

Now, halfway through what had turned into one of our busiest days of the year, I could hear her chattering with customers out front. Her voice carried that infectious enthusiasm that drew people in, made them want to be part of whatever she was creating. The bell above the door chimed every few minutes, bringing in another wave of holiday shoppers drawn by her window display.

The sound should have been grating after hours of it, but instead it felt like a heartbeat, the rhythm of a normal life I'd fought so hard to build.

Her excitement had been infectious when she showed me the space she'd cleared for my leather work—prime real estate near the register, with proper display backlighting and everything. She'd rearranged the store to make it happen, her hyper-focus channeled into creating the perfect display space.

"Your stuff is too good to hide in the back room," she'd declared, her rainbow glasses slipping down her nose. Her purple micro braids had been freshly done, wrapped in two thick bubble plaits that swung with her enthusiasm. The oversized cardigan she wore—today's featuring panels of knitted celestial patterns—had nearly knocked over a display of vintage teacups in her excitement. "And don't argue about the profit split. You earned it."

The shop bell chimed again, and something in me recognized the presence before I even looked up. Power rolled through the store like a summer storm, making the hair on the back of my neck stand up. My hands stilled on the leather, fingers pressing into the soft hide hard enough to leave impressions of my fingerprints. The temperature dropped and rose all at once, like the moment before lightning strikes.

Kronos.

Here.

In the daylight.

The winter light caught his perfectly styled red quiff as he stepped into the shop, transforming ordinary copper into something ethereal. Those silver eyes—quicksilver pools that captured both starlight and storm clouds—swept across the room until they found mine, and time seemed to slow. His brown leather jacket hung on broad shoulders with the casual confidence that only true old money could affect, its worn edges somehow making the pristine clothing beneath appear even more expensive. The shadow of stubble along his jaw invited thoughts of how it might feel against my fingertips, my cheek, my lips—a deliberate contrast to the aristocratic lines of his face.

My heart lurched against my ribs as recognition hit. The alleyway behind The Rusty Nail. The taste of whiskey on his lips. My knees on rough concrete. The breathless invitation to his apartment that had sent me fleeing into the night. I hadn't expected to ever see him again—I'd convinced myself that in the bar's darkness I wouldn't even recognize him if I did. There was no mistaking that face, even in the unforgiving daylight.

I heard Twyla's cheerful greeting float back from the front of the store: "Welcome to Twyla's Trinket & Trade! Let me know if you need any help finding—" Her voice caught, and I knew she'd felt it too. That otherness that rolled off him in waves. She possessed an almost supernatural awareness of the unseen currents of life, the emotions of others, and the spirit of places. It's why her window displays always caught the right light, or why customers felt so at home in her chaos.

My heart hammered against my ribs, keeping time with the nervous tapping of my fingers against the workbench. I'd left cum drunk and dazed, like a quickie in an alley was supposed to end. I hadn't expected him to track me down here. He hunted people for a living, for christ's sake!

I forced myself to keep sorting, to maintain the pretense of normalcy even as my body remembered how his hands had felt, how he tasted—

"Interesting selection of merchandise you have here," his voice carried from the front, that strange accent making every word sound like dark honey. "But I'm looking for something specific."

"Oh? What can I help you find?" Twyla's voice held none of its usual pep. Sometimes I forgot that under all that creative chaos was a shrewd businesswoman who'd built this place from the ground up.

"I believe you have a leather worker on staff. Is he available?"

My fingers slipped on the awl I'd been pretending to clean, piercing my palm. The metal was cold, grounding. A weapon, if I needed it—though against whatever supernatural thing Kronos was, it would be as effective as throwing paper clips at a freight train.

"Alex?" Twyla's voice carried back to my workspace. Protecting me in her way. Giving me the choice to answer or not. I could stay silent, but the prickle along my spine told me Kronos already knew where I was. "Alex?" Twyla called again, her voice carrying a question. I took a steadying breath and stepped out from my workspace, forcing myself to move with a confidence I didn't feel.

"Can I help you?"

Kronos's smile was slow, his gaze taking me in. "I believe you dropped something in your haste to get away from me last night."

My stomach dropped. During that rushed encounter in the dark alley, had I—? My hands instinctively went to my back pocket. Empty. My wallet. It must have fallen when I'd dropped to my knees.

"Oh!" Twyla's voice cut through the memory. "Alex, why didn't you tell me you lost your wallet? I could have helped you look for it." Her concern was genuine, but there was something else in her tone. Caution, maybe. She'd positioned herself between us, pretending to rearrange the display items.

"Oh. I hadn't realized I'd lost it." I managed, my voice steadier than I felt. I couldn't look away from Kronos—the way his suit jacket pulled across his shoulders as he leaned against the counter, casual as a cat in the sun.

Twyla's hands never stopped moving, but her body was tense. "Well, lucky it was found then." She glanced between us, no doubt catching the tension crackling in the air. "Though I have to wonder how you knew where to return it."

Kronos's laugh was low and rich, like aged whiskey. "I have my ways." His eyes caught mine, amusement dancing in their depths. "Though your workplace being listed on your ID made it easier than usual."

The employee ID card Twyla had insisted on making for me, complete with the shop's address in flowing script. I'd tucked it behind my driver's license months ago and forgotten about it.

"I see," Twyla said, as she straightened a display of vintage brooches with deliberate focus. "Well, I need to check on some inventory in the back. Alex, you can handle things out here?" The question was loaded—she was offering me an out.

"Don't worry *mi amor*, I've got it covered," I said, proud that my voice remained steady despite the way my pulse jumped when Kronos shifted closer, closing the careful distance I'd tried to maintain. Kronos looked between us.

Her lips twitched before she disappeared into the back room, her footsteps fading down the hall. Kronos leaned across the counter, his calloused fingers circling my wrist with a grip that was both gentle and unyielding. The warmth of his breath against my ear sent shivers down my spine, and I caught the faintest hint of his cologne—something woodsy and masculine that made my head spin in the crisp morning air.

Chapter Four

WICKED

The shop had quieted for the night, but my nerves were anything but calm. For the hundredth time today, I pulled up the new message window on my phone, staring at the number I'd saved from that damn business card. The cursor blinked mockingly as I deleted yet another attempt at a casual first text.

"Still composing your masterpiece?" Twyla's voice drifted from behind the counter where she was counting down the register. I could hear the smirk without looking up.

"I'm not—" I protested, but my fingers were already typing again.

Alex: *Hi. It's Alex. Does this count as a ring?*

My thumb hovered over the send button. Was it too cheesy? Too forward? Not forward enough? I'd been second-guessing myself since yesterday morning when he—

"Incoming!" Twyla called out. Before I could process her warning, she 'accidentally' bumped into me with a box of new inventory. My phone jerked in my hand, thumb hitting send before I could stop it.

"*¡Ay, mierda!*" I muttered, staring at the delivered confirmation in horror.

"Oops, did I do that?" Twyla's innocent tone wouldn't have fooled anyone, least of all me. Her dark purple nails, adorned with intricate golden runes, drummed against the box she was still holding. "Well, thank god for that. You've only rewritten that text about a thousand times."

Heat crawled up my neck. "You saw that?"

"Honey, everyone in a three-block radius has seen you agonizing over that text."

"He probably won't even respond," I said, trying to sound casual and failing miserably.

She snorted, setting down the box. "That gorgeous man that couldn't take his eyes off you? Who touched you every chance he got? If you don't want him, send him my way."

ZZZ ZZZ! My phone vibrated.

My stomach did a backflip worthy of an Olympic gymnast.

"Ooh, is that him?" Twyla practically bounced over. "What did he say?"

My hands were shaking too much to even unlock the screen. "What do I do?"

Twyla rolled her eyes and plucked the phone from my fingers. "Huh," she grinned. "He's confident, I'll give him that."

"*Que?*" I lunged for the phone. "What does it say?" She released it with a flourish.

Kronos: *Le Coucou's on 11th. 8pm tonight. Dress nice, it's a classy place.*
- Kronos Orestes

"Oh shit," Twyla said, looking up through her oversized glasses at her phone. "That's in an hour. You better get moving."

"What? No, I can't—it's my turn to close, and we still have to—"

"I've got this." She was already shoving me toward the back stairs that led to my apartment. "Go. Wear that blue button-up—it brings out your eyes."

"Twyla—"

"Move it! I'm not letting you use inventory as an excuse to duck your date."

My stomach twisted at her words. I wasn't hiding. I just...didn't do this part. Hookups were easy—clinical, almost. This was something else entirely.

I forced myself to type "See you there" before jumping into the shower. Steam filled the bathroom as I tackled my hair—a constant battle of dark, thick waves that refused to cooperate. After what felt like forever, I finally got it looking intentionally tousled rather than just messy. A careful shave, a splash of the good cologne, and several wardrobe changes later, I was sprinting down the sidewalk, already cutting it close. My breath fogged in the frigid evening air, and I tugged my coat tighter against the biting wind that whipped between the buildings.

Le Coucou loomed ahead, all elegant lighting and expensive cars parked out front. The hairs on the back of my neck stood up before I heard him.

"I thought you wouldn't make it."

A wisp of steam curled from his words in the freezing night air as Kronos stepped into the warm glow of the street lamp. He looked devastating in a charcoal suit that fit him like sin, his red hair catching the light like a dark flame.

My body remembered two nights ago—the brick wall rough against my palms, his hands in my hair, the way he'd groaned my name in that filthy alley. Sex was familiar territory. Easy. Safe, in its own way. The way he was looking at me now, like he could see past every defense I'd built, like he was after something far more precious than physical pleasure... that made my mouth go dry. I wanted to run.

"Traffic," I said, though my voice came out ragged.

A knowing smirk played at the corner of his mouth. "Of course." His eyes dragged over me slowly, deliberately. "Blue suits you." The way he looked at me turned my knees to Jell-O.

My cheeks burned, not from shame—I'd left shame behind years ago—but from the raw intimacy of his gaze. The rush of warm air inside was a stark contrast to the December chill, and my cold cheeks began to thaw as we followed the maître d' through the elegant space. It was impossible to focus on anything but Kronos.

He set his menu down after barely glancing at it. I was still deliberating between the duck and the lamb when the waitress returned. Before I could speak, Kronos's voice cut through the air: "He'll have the duck confit with the wild mushroom risotto. I'll take the ribeye, rare." He didn't even look at her as he handed over both menus. "And bring us the 2015 Château Margaux."

"I can order for myself," I said once she'd left, irritation warring with an unexpected flutter in my stomach—he'd chosen exactly what I'd been leaning toward.

His lips quirked up as he lifted his wine glass. "I'm sure you can." The red wine caught the light like liquid garnets as he took a slow sip. "But you'll find I have a knack for knowing what people want."

Heat crept up my neck. "Is that so?" I tried to keep my tone light, playful. "Then why did you ask me here? What do I want?"

"Technically," he set down his glass with deliberate precision, "you asked me. But as for what you want..." His eyes darkened. "I think you want the same thing I do. A game."

"A game?"

"I have specific tastes." He leaned forward, making the world fade away. "I think you'll enjoy them. You see, I'm going to hunt you." His voice dropped lower, intimate. "You're going to run. If I catch you—" his lips curved into a predatory smile "—I fuck you in every way your little bunny brain can handle. Until you're a trembling, dripping mess that can't so much as whisper 'thank you.'" He sat back, casual as ever. "You get ten minutes to hide anywhere in the city. Then, I'm coming for you."

A shiver ran down my spine—fear or arousal, I couldn't tell. Maybe both. I forced a laugh. "You're not serious."

"Deadly." The word hung between us like a promise. He gestured to my plate as our food arrived. "Eat. You'll need your energy." The conversation shifted then, becoming lighter, filled with subtle flirtation and shared laughter. By dessert, I'd almost convinced myself he'd been joking. That this was just an elaborate form of foreplay.

Then we stepped out into the alley beside the restaurant.

Before I could react, my back hit the brick wall. His mouth crashed into mine, hungry and demanding. His hands were everywhere at once—tangling in my hair, gripping my hip, sliding under my shirt to trace burning patterns on my skin. I melted into him, forgetting everything but the heat building between us.

Then he pulled back, just enough to look down into my eyes. His breath was hot against my ear as he whispered one word: "Run."

Something electric shot through me—primal, instinctive. Before I could think, my feet were already moving, carrying me deeper into the night, the icy air burning in my lungs as I ran. Behind me, I heard his dark chuckle echo off the alley walls.

34

Chapter Five

HUNTED

Ten minutes. That's what he'd given me—ten minutes to lose myself in a city I thought I knew. The cold bit into my lungs as I ran, each breath crystallizing in the winter air.

My dress shoes slipped on black ice as I rounded another corner. I caught sight of him ahead and spun down Mason Avenue—only to spot that distinctive red hair near the entrance to Twilight Lane. Impossible. He'd been behind me. I took the only other option—deeper into the maze of historic homes where old money and older magic lived in ornate facades.

The streets grew quieter here, more residential. Gas lamps still cast long shadows across cobblestone streets. Each turn led further into the heart of the district, past towering Victorian mansions.

My foot caught on uneven stone as I passed an imposing brownstone. I went down hard on the bottom steps; the impact driving what little air remained from my lungs. Cold began seeping through my clothes as I tried and failed to push myself up. Through blurred vision, I took in the building's commanding presence—old stone and gleaming brass, elaborate ironwork framing a door that looked like it belonged in another century.

In the strange half-light of the gas lamps, I could see my breath coming in short, desperate clouds.

"I found you." His voice rolled through the darkness like thunder, equal parts amusement and hunger. "Are you ready to play?"

Pain shot through my ribs as I tried to push myself up from the cold stone steps. Even breathing hurt, the freezing air burning in my overworked lungs.

"Need a hand?" His voice was rich with amusement. When I didn't answer, his fingers tangled in my hair. Not pulling—not yet—but establishing control. "Or should I carry you?"

"I can walk," I managed, though my legs felt like jelly. His hand slid from my hair to grip my upper arm, hauling me to my feet with effortless strength. The world spun as blood rushed to my head.

"Of course you can." He steadied me, one large hand settling at the small of my back. The warmth of his palm seeped through my sweat-damp shirt. "Though I have to wonder if you know where you've run to."

In the light from the old gas lamps, the brownstone loomed like something from another century. Intricate ironwork framed a door that weighed more than I did, brass fixtures gleaming despite the late hour.

A slow smile spread across his face as understanding dawned in my eyes. "Darling bunny. You ran straight home to me." Dark amusement coloring his voice as he ushered me inside. I'd expected a sparse bachelor pad, maybe a studio apartment above one of the shops like mine. What I got instead was one of the renovated Victorian mansions that lined the historic district. Kronos guided me through a heavy wooden door, his hand never leaving the small of my back.

The foyer opened into a space that looked like it belonged in a magazine spread—warm-toned hardwood floors and high coffered ceilings. A massive leather sectional dominated one wall, its rich burgundy surface gleaming in the light from art *déco* sconces. The coffee table looked carved from a single piece of ancient wood, its surface rippling with natural whorls and knots that moved in the shadowy light.

Massive canvases lined the walls, all in rich colors that absorbed the light. One depicted a hunt scene—dark figures on horseback pursuing something just out of frame, their forms almost liquid in their movement. Another showed what might have been a forest at night, but the longer I looked at it, the more the branches seemed to reach out from the canvas, twisting into almost-familiar shapes.

"Nice place," I managed, trying not to stare at a striking piece that appeared to be painted in shades of dried blood. "Bounty hunting must pay better than I thought."

Kronos chuckled, the sound reverberating through his chest where he'd pressed against my back. "I've been at it a long time." His lips brushed my ear. "Very long." I shivered, and not just from the contact. There was something about this place—something in the way the shadows pooled in the corners, in the way the art seemed to watch us.

"Drink?" He was already moving toward a bar cart that looked like it belonged in an old-world gentleman's club, all polished brass and cut crystal.

"Dark 'n' Stormy?"

He paused, considering me with an expression I couldn't quite read. "I have something else in mind. Something special." He lifted a decanter filled with a clear liquid that shimmered with an opalescent glow. "Family recipe."

I shifted uncomfortably under his gaze. "What is it?"

"An old Primal tradition." He poured a small measure into a crystal glass, the liquid catching the light like moonlight on water. "My ancestors used it during hunts."

"Hunts?" Something in his tone made me wary. "As in...hunting people?"

He nodded, his expression serious now. "In the old days, yes. The drink heightens sensation, makes everything more intense. They gave it to prey to disorient them, make the chase more...interesting." He held the glass up, studying how the liquid clung to the crystal. "It's harmless, but the sensory effects are quite powerful."

My mouth went dry. "And you want me to drink that?"

"Only if you choose to." He set the glass down between us, not pushing it toward me. "I don't give it lightly, and never without explanation. The choice is yours."

I stared at the shimmering liquid, trying to process what he was telling me. "Why offer it to me at all?"

"Because I want you to experience pleasure the way I can give it." His voice dropped lower.

"What will it feel like?" I asked, fingers hovering near the glass but not touching it.

"Every sensation amplified. My touch will feel deeper, more intense. Pleasure becomes...transcendent."

I considered him for a long moment. This man who could have deceived me. He could have just given me the drink and I'd have been none the wiser.

"I'll try it," I said, reaching for the glass.

His approving smile felt like sunshine. "Just a small sip first. Let's see how it affects you."

The first taste glided across my tongue—smoke and starlight, if starlight had a taste. Warmth bloomed in my chest, spreading like liquid fire through my veins, chasing away the ache in my ribs. Every nerve ending felt alive, yet I remained clear-headed, aware. "*¡Eso está del carajo!*"

"Told you we could do better than that mind numbing tar." He watched me, gauging my reaction. "How do you feel?"

"Like my skin is awake," I admitted, fascinated by the beat of my heart, stronger and more present than before. "But I still feel...like me."

"That's the point," he said, something like pride in his voice. "Heightened, not controlled. I want you to be aware of what comes next." He took a step closer, and I couldn't help backing up until my legs hit the leather sofa. His free hand came up to trace my jawline, the touch sending sparks of electricity dancing across my skin. His thumb brushed over my pulse point, and I couldn't suppress a shiver. "The bruising's already fading."

The pain was gone, replaced by a tingling sensitivity that made even the brush of my shirt feel intense.

"Who are you?" The words came out breathier than I intended.

His smile widened, showing teeth that were sharper than they'd been at the restaurant. "Exactly who you're looking for."

Chapter Six

Sweet Surrender

My breath caught as he crowded me against the sofa, one hand sliding into my hair. The other gripped my hip, his thumb finding skin where my shirt had ridden up. Even that small touch sent goosebumps skittering across my skin.

"What exactly am I looking for?"

"Someone stronger than you." His fingers tightened in my hair, pulling my head back to expose my throat. The slight pain mixed with pleasure, drawing a moan from deep in my chest. My mind flickered between surrender and resistance—I'd never let anyone manhandle me like this before, yet my body responded with an eagerness that shocked me. The vulnerability of my exposed throat should have terrified me, but it felt like release.

"To know every inch of you." Kronos' lips brushed my neck, his tongue swirling over my pounding pulse. I could feel my heartbeat against his mouth, hammering so hard I was sure he could taste my anticipation. Each point of contact was overwhelming, like he was lighting up circuits in my body I hadn't known existed. The room seemed to fade around us, my focus narrowing to just his touch, his scent, the heat of his breath against my skin.

Kronos slid his rough fingers under my shirt, burning hot against my over-sensitized skin. The contrast between the cool leather beneath me and his scorching touch made me shiver. I'd been touched before, but never like this. This focused intensity that made me feel both seen and consumed at once.

"Someone who can make you forget everything else."

God help me, I wanted to forget—to let go of the constant vigilance, the armor I'd built around myself piece by painful piece. For once, I wanted to stop being the one in control, the one responsible for protecting myself. The realization flooded me with equal parts terror and desire. Could I surrender to him? Did I even remember how to let go?

I arched into him, desperate for more contact. My hands found their way under the edge of his jeans, cupping his ass and giving it a firm squeeze. "Promises, promises."

He growled, and I was on my back on the sofa, his weight pinning me down. The leather felt soothingly cool against my burning skin.

"I always keep my promises." His voice was rough, deeper than before, the words resonating somewhere primal inside me. He caught my wrists in one large hand, pinning them above my head with an effortless strength that made my breath catch in my throat. The position left me exposed to his touch, defenseless in a way that should have triggered all my alarms. I'd spent years ensuring no one could trap me, control me—yet here I was, willingly caught.

I tested his grip, a reflexive resistance that melted into acceptance when I couldn't break free. Heat pooled low in my stomach, an unexpected thrill racing through me at the realization of how completely he had me at his mercy. This wasn't like the Madam's control that had left me feeling hollow and used—this was something I craved, something I was choosing despite every instinct screaming that vulnerability meant danger.

His free hand traced patterns on my skin that left trails of fire in their wake, each touch deliberate and possessive. It was as if Kronos was mapping me, learning the topography of my body through careful exploration. The gentleness behind his firm grip confused and excited me, making me arch into his touch despite myself. I was trapped between the need to protect myself and the desperate desire to surrender.

"Prove it."

His answering smile was all teeth. His grip tightened on my wrists as he leaned down, breath hot against my ear. "Last chance to say no," he murmured, teeth grazing my earlobe.

"Please," I gasped. The suffocating pressure of reality closed in—recollections of hands that grabbed without permission, of gazes that focused only on what I could provide, of my father's voice repeating I would never measure up. It was all right there, a tidal wave threatening to drown me, clawing at the edges of this moment.

The weight of the world bore down, suffocating me with every breath I didn't surrender to him. My skin crawled with phantom touches from people who'd used me, my ears rang with the Madam's laughter, my chest ached with the certainty that I was damaged beyond repair. I needed it gone, needed it silenced.

Here, pinned beneath this beautiful, dangerous creature, I could feel the darkness receding with each touch, each controlled breath. Nothing else existed in the space between us but this raw, consuming need.

"Make me forget," I begged, the words torn from somewhere primal inside me. I needed oblivion. I needed to disappear into this feeling before I shattered.

He cupped my face, thumb brushing across my lower lip. "Let go," his voice sounded like smoke. "Let me take control."

I closed my eyes, surrendering to him. The room darkened around us; the paintings moving in my peripheral vision. His mouth found my throat again, alternating between sharp bites and soothing kisses until I was incoherent.

"That's it," he breathed against my throat, one hand sliding down my body with deliberate slowness. "I've got you, pet." His hand slid under my shirt, calluses catching on my skin as he traced up my ribs. I had to bite my lip to keep from yelping.

"So sensitive," Kronos growled, finding my nipple and twisting it between rough fingers. A sharp jolt of pleasure shot straight to my groin. He pinched harder, and I heard myself make a sound I'd never made before. My hands strained against his iron grip above my head, needing to touch him, to anchor myself as sensation rippled through me.

My body betrayed me. I'd always kept control with clients, faking the right responses. Some of them felt okay enough to finish…but never anything like this. I shook beneath him, every muscle quivering, completely at his mercy. The surrender terrified me and turned me on more than anything I'd ever felt.

"Please," I begged, pride shattered, replaced by naked hunger. The scratch of his beard abraded my throat, his touch ghosted down my stomach, his thigh pressed hard against my aching shaft. I couldn't focus on anything but where he touched me, everything else vanishing into meaningless darkness.

"What do you need, pet?" His voice poured like liquid sin directly into my ear. The word 'pet' burrowed into me, possessive and thrilling. His teeth caught my earlobe and bit down, the sharp sting yanking me back to reality for just a second before his fingers dipped beneath my waistband and dragged me under again.

His fingertips traced patterns just below my navel, skimming beneath the fabric—teasing, maddening, withholding what I needed. My hips bucked upward, chasing his touch like a starving man chased food.

"Patience," he commanded, the word rumbling from his chest into mine. That voice compelled obedience, reaching into me and pulling out surrender I didn't know I had to give. His mouth latched onto that secret spot behind my ear he'd discovered, sucking hard, marking me as his. The thought of wearing his mark tomorrow sent a rush flooding through me.

He finally—finally—slid his hand lower. I gasped his name, the word torn from my throat. The ruthless suction at my neck contrasted with the teasing lightness of his fingers so close to where I needed them, my mind splitting between the twin sensations.

He played my body like an instrument he'd spent years mastering, pushing me to the edge where pleasure became almost unbearable before backing off just enough to keep me desperate. When I thought I might die if he didn't touch me properly, he'd change tactics, starting the torturous climb again. No one had ever read me so perfectly, breaking through every defense I'd built to keep people from seeing what I really wanted.

"Look at me," Kronos commanded, and I forced my eyes open to meet that molten silver gaze. The hunger I saw there made me shudder. "I want to watch you fall apart."

He slid his fingers from base to tip with a featherlight touch.

"Please," the word broke on a moan as his thumb circled just right. My wrists strained against his grip, but he held me in place.

"Don't move," Kronos crooned into my neck. My whole body shuddered at the command in his voice. His fingers kept up that torturous rhythm, each touch precise and devastating. His kiss swallowed my whimpers, his tongue mimicking the rhythm of his hand until I couldn't think.

Kronos' teeth caught my lower lip as his fingers worked me higher. The ecstasy built in waves, each stroke making me arch and gasp beneath him. I couldn't think past the feeling of his hand, his mouth, the weight of him keeping me exactly where he wanted me.

"That's it," he murmured against my lips. His thumb pressed harder, circling in a way that made stars explode behind my eyes. "Let me hear you."

The sound that escaped me wasn't even words anymore. His fingers moved faster, more demanding, the pleasure building until I thought I might break from it.

"Kronos," I gasped, trembling on the edge. "I can't—"

"You can," he growled, and the command in his voice broke something loose inside me. "cum for me, bunny."

My entire body seized as pleasure ripped through me, every nerve ending singing with bliss. Heat bloomed in my core and exploded outward until my skin felt like it was on fire. My thighs trembled, toes curling as waves of ecstasy pulsed through me again and again. Each stroke of his fingers drew out another wave until I couldn't tell where one ended and the next began. I couldn't remember anything except how to feel. The intensity built until my mind went blank, my back arching off the leather as my body spasmed with release.

The world dissolved into warm, velvet darkness. I floated there, peaceful and blank, unable to remember how to form words. Nothing existed except the comforting void and distant sensations of heat and weight against my skin.

A deep voice rumbled through me, though I couldn't make out the words at first. Time didn't exist here in the darkness—I could have been floating for seconds or hours before meaning started to filter through. Everything felt soft and hazy, my body light and tingling.

"Breathe for me, bunny." The command penetrated the fog, and I sucked in a shaky breath, then another, each one bringing me closer to reality. "That's it. Come back to me." Gentle fingers stroked my face, the touch grounding me to my body. "Open those beautiful eyes."

My eyelids felt heavy, and I struggled to obey. When I managed it, his face filled my vision, that devastating mouth curved in a soft smile. The pad of his thumb brushed over my cheek, catching errant wetness. I tried to speak, to thank him, but my tongue wouldn't cooperate. All I could manage was a soft, broken sound as aftershocks of pleasure still rippled through me.

"Welcome back," he murmured, those calloused fingers still stroking my face. Every touch sent little sparks through my oversensitive skin. His other hand moved to my chest, palm flat against my thundering heart. "Keep breathing for me."

The world filtered back slowly—scents of leather and cedar, the weight of him against me, distant sounds of traffic through the windows. My hands were still stretched above my head, fingers tingling as circulation returned. When I tried to move them, my muscles protested the change.

He caught my clumsy attempt, guiding my arms down with careful attention. His fingers worked over my wrists, the gentle massage drawing a soft sound from my throat. "Easy," he said, pressing soft kisses to the tender skin there. "Let me take care of you."

I wanted to tell him I was fine, that I didn't need taking care of, but my mouth still wouldn't form words. He gathered me against his chest, and I melted into his warmth, my head tucked under his chin.

He held me like that until my breathing steadied, a hand running slow circles across my shoulders. The cotton of his shirt felt soft against my cheek. When he shifted, I made a sound of protest that would have embarrassed me if I'd had the energy to care.

"Just getting you more comfortable," he murmured, lips brushing my temple. He repositioned us on the sofa, my body draped over his chest. The throw blanket he pulled over us was silk-soft against my skin.

His fingers carded through my hair in a way that made my eyes flutter closed. "Think you can drink something for me?" When I managed a small nod, he reached for what looked like crystal on the side table. "Small sips."

The rim of the glass pressed against my lips. The liquid was cool and sweet—not the strange drink from earlier, just water, but it felt like heaven on my parched throat. His other hand never stopped its gentle movements in my hair.

When I'd managed a few sips, he set the glass aside. Everything felt soft and hazy, my body melting further into his warmth with each gentle touch. The steady thrum of his heartbeat under my ear grounded me to the moment.

"You did so well for me," he praised. The words sparked something warm in my stomach. My fingers curled into his shirt, holding on as if he might disappear.

Time moved strangely—I might have dozed, floating in and out of awareness to find his hands still moving in soothing patterns across my skin. At some point, rich scents of chocolate and fruit teased my senses.

"You need to eat something." His voice drew me back from the edge of sleep. "Just a little." When I opened my eyes, I found him holding what looked like a piece of expensive dark chocolate.

He pressed the chocolate against my lips, and the decadent taste bloomed across my tongue. The simple act of letting him feed me should have felt strange, but in this soft, floating headspace, it felt natural.

"There you are," he murmured as awareness slowly returned to my eyes. A sip of water followed the chocolate, then what tasted like fresh strawberries. Each bite was offered with infinite patience, his touch remaining gentle.

The room felt different now, less threatening. The leather beneath had warmed to our body heat. I shifted, testing muscles that felt pleasantly worn.

"How are you feeling?" he asked, thumb brushing over my chin to catch a drop of water.

I had to swallow twice before I could find my voice. "Like I'm floating."

The world still felt soft at the edges when Kronos helped me up from the couch. My legs were shaky, and he steadied me with a hand on my lower back as he guided me through the house.

The bathroom took my breath away—all marble and antique brass fixtures, with a massive claw-foot tub that could have fit four people. Steam already rose from the water, carrying the scent of luxury bath oils. The soft light from art déco sconces made the polished surfaces glow.

He helped me into the warm water first, his hands steady and sure. I sank into the heat with a contented sigh, letting it soothe my sore muscles.

The water shifted as Kronos slid in behind me, and I tensed for a moment before his hands found my shoulders. Strong fingers worked into the knots there, drawing a low moan of appreciation from my throat. I relaxed back against the solid warmth of his chest.

The water shifted with each measured movement of his hands, tiny ripples catching the soft light. I melted further into his touch, head falling forward as his thumbs worked along my spine. His breath stirred the damp hair at my nape. Shame crept in at the edges of my pleasure.

I bit my lip hard, trying to focus on the physical sensation rather than the voice in my head. *Undeserving. Worthless. Taking advantage.* The pressure of Kronos's thumbs found a knot of tension, and I gasped, the pain-pleasure silencing my self-loathing. I didn't know how to accept this tenderness without questioning it, without waiting for the moment he'd realize I wasn't worth the effort. My shoulders tensed under his touch.

"You're thinking too much," he whispered in my ear, as if he could read the battle in my mind. His hands never stopped their methodical work, pressing into muscles that had forgotten how to relax. No one had ever just touched me to make me feel good, not without expecting something in return. What would he want later? What would be the price for this moment of care?

I shifted, and his breath caught. The slight movement made me very aware of his arousal pressed against me. His hands stilled on my waist. "Tonight is all about you. This proximity has its side effects, but don't feel pressured to do more."

"I want to," I breathed, pressing back against him. His grip tightened, fingers digging into my hips, drawing a sharp gasp from my throat.

His lips traced down my neck as his hand spread across my stomach, pinning me against him. "Tell me if it's too much," he said, his voice rough with restraint as he began a slow, deliberate rhythm against me. The hard length of him slid between my thighs, teasing what we both wanted.

Each roll of his hips sent water crashing against the edges of the tub. His mouth worked along my shoulder, leaving a trail of bites and kisses that made my skin prickle with anticipation. I felt marked, claimed, even before he was inside me.

"Is this okay?" he asked, his breath hot against my ear. The shape of him pressed insistently against me, impossibly hard.

"Yes," I said, reaching back to grab his hair, pulling hard enough to hurt. The motion made me arch against him, my back bowing. The sound he made wasn't human—a primal growl that vibrated through my entire body. "Please…"

He positioned himself, one hand still splayed across my stomach while the other guided him to my entrance. The first push breached me slowly, deliberately. The stretch burned in the best way—painful and perfect. I hadn't done this in almost a year.

I gasped for air as he continued pushing in, my body struggling to accommodate him. His free hand moved to my chest, fingers finding my nipple and pinching just hard enough to distract me from the initial discomfort.

His hips stilled once he was fully seated inside me. I felt impaled, stretched to my limits, my body adjusting to the intrusion. The water made everything slicker, more intense, amplifying every tiny movement.

I forced air into my lungs as he pushed inside me, stretching me wider than I'd been in months. Fuck, he was big—bigger than I remembered from just feeling him in my mouth.

His fingers bruised my hips, holding me steady while I adjusted. I clenched around him, drawing a deep groan from his throat that vibrated through my back. The water lapped against us, turning every tiny movement into something fluid and intense. I rolled my hips, testing him, and nearly sobbed when he hit that spot inside me.

"My gorgeous, perfect pet," he growled, his lips against my neck, teeth scraping my skin. The possessiveness in his voice made me clench around him. He guided me into a rhythm that had water sloshing over the edge with each thrust. Every time he drove into me, stars burst behind my eyes.

His grip shifted without warning. His hands slid under my thighs, hooking beneath my knees and spreading my legs wide apart. He lifted me up, water streaming down my body, leaving me completely exposed with my legs forced open. Helpless. On display. He held me suspended above him, my weight nothing to his inhuman strength. The absolute control he had over me should have triggered panic. Instead, I went slack in his hands, my head falling back onto his shoulder. I wanted him to take all of me.

My orgasm hit without mercy. My cock spurted untouched, cum mixing with bathwater as my body convulsed around him.

"God, oh fuck—"

Kronos tightened his grip, fingers digging into the sensitive skin behind my knees as he slammed me down hard onto him. He came inside me with a growl that sounded barely human, his teeth sinking into my shoulder hard enough to mark. The pain mixed with the aftershocks of my orgasm, prolonging it until I thought I might black out.

My muscles gave out as he lowered us back into the water. My limbs felt disconnected, my mind floating somewhere above us. Kronos held me against his chest, his arms still strong despite what we'd just done. His lips brushed my temple—so gentle compared to the way he'd just fucked me senseless. That softness made my chest ache in ways I couldn't handle right now.

The steady thud of his heart beneath my ear and the water lapping at our cooling skin pulled me toward sleep. I tried to stay awake, to savor this strange peace I felt in his arms, but exhaustion dragged me under. As darkness took me, I felt his fingers combing through my wet hair. For the first time in years, I fell asleep feeling completely safe in someone else's arms.

Chapter Seven

MORNING AFTER NEVER

ZZZ ZZZ! The muffled sound of my phone dragged me out of a deep sleep. I blinked groggily—Egyptian cotton whispered against my skin as I shifted, their rich gold color catching the morning light streaming through floor-to-ceiling windows. The mattress felt like sleeping on a cloud, nothing like my bargain store special.

Memory rushed back as I blindly reached for my phone, and my heart stopped. Ten missed calls from Twyla. *Fuck.* A flood of unread texts that started concerned and grew increasingly panicked. On top of that, I was already an hour late for work. The last message made my stomach drop: "Alex, if you don't answer in the next hour I'm calling the police."

"Shit, shit, shit." I scrambled up, wincing at muscles I didn't even know could be sore. My clothes sat in a neat, folded stack on a plush armchair by the window—definitely not how I'd left them strewn across the floor last night. Someone—Kronos presumably—had even taken the time to smooth out the wrinkles in my dress shirt. The fire escape outside the window caught my eye, and without letting myself think too hard about it, I was dressed and climbing out. No awkward morning-after conversation necessary.

The metal grating was freezing under my hands as I made my way down, trying not to think about how many stories up we were. My shoes were not made for this, and I slipped twice on patches of frost. The last ladder dropped me into an alley between two dumpsters, and I dodged a cluster of violet-eyed rats that scattered at my approach.

I burst through the shop's front door twenty minutes later, the bell's cheerful chime at odds with the way every customer turned to stare. Mrs. Henderson, one of our regular antique browsers, actually clutched her pearls. The teenager trying on steampunk goggles snickered behind her hand. Only then did I catch my reflection in the sunglasses display mirror—rumpled dress shirt despite Kronos's careful folding, hair sticking up at odd angles, and...were those bite marks already turning purple along my collar?

"Go get cleaned up," Twyla said from behind the register, her voice carrying that rare note of professional disappointment that was worse than anger. "We'll talk later." She was dressed in one of her signature oversized cardigans, this one featuring patches of different textile patterns sewn together like a fabric collage. Her purple micro braids were wrapped in an elaborate crown today, decorated with tiny brass gears that caught the light as she turned back to her customer.

I took the stairs two at a time up to my apartment, grateful that at least my keys had still been in my pocket. The shower barely had time to get warm before I was out again, rushing through my morning routine. As I passed the full-length mirror in my bedroom, I froze. My body was a canvas of marks—teeth impressions scattered across my chest, finger-shaped bruises on my hips, evidence of last night painted across my skin like some debauched art piece.

Fuck. I traced a bruise where his thumb had dug into my hip. Just one night and I'd let him mark me like this? So goddamn easy, just like my father always said. One smooth-talking man with a nice smile and I'd melted, invited him into not just my bed but under my skin. The worst part was how much I'd wanted it, how I'd begged for more. *Pathetic.*

I pressed against a purple bite mark on my collarbone, watching my reflection wince. The pain should have disgusted me, should have been a warning to stay away. Instead, it sent a treacherous shiver of desire through me. What kind of messed-up person gets turned on by being treated like this? The kind who'd worked at Ogygia, clearly. Maybe the Madam had ruined me for normal after all.

He'd washed my hair afterward…and the way he'd checked each mark with careful fingers, asking if I was okay? That tenderness confused me more than the bruises. Monsters aren't supposed to be gentle. It was easier to hate him, to cast him as the villain who'd taken advantage of my weakness. The alternative was too dangerous to contemplate.

I opted for a black turtleneck, trying not to think about why those marks made heat pool in my stomach despite my resentment. The soft wool was both comfort and torment against my sensitized skin. Comfortable jeans and boots completed the outfit, the everyday normality of the clothes a shield against the chaos he'd introduced into my life. I couldn't afford to get attached to someone like him. I'd been down that road before, and it only ended one way—with me broken and alone while they moved on to easier prey. No...I'd lose his number and just move on.

The day dragged on endlessly. I rang up Mrs. Peterson's usual collection of antique thimbles, helped a teenager find the perfect steampunk goggles for her costume, and sorted through three boxes of consignment jewelry that Twyla had accepted without checking for quality. Every time I bent down to reach the lower shelf display, a delicious ache reminded me of last night.

The high neck of my sweater rubbed against the constellation of bite marks Kronos had left, each brush of fabric sending my mind straight back to his bedroom. Halfway through cataloging a new shipment, I stared at the same pocket watch for five minutes, lost in the memory of his hands pinning my wrists above my head. I dropped an entire tray of vintage timepieces when my brain supplied the exact sound he'd made when he came, causing Mr. Daniels to ask if I was feeling feverish since my face had gone "redder than a summer tomato."

The winter sun was setting by the time the last customer left, casting long shadows through Twyla's elaborate window display. She'd changed it again while I was gone—the paper snowflakes replaced with crystalline branches that caught the fading light, casting rainbow patterns across the floor.

"Office. Now." Her tone brooked no argument as she flipped the sign to CLOSED. The door had barely clicked shut before she threw her arms around me, the brass gears in her hair jingling. "Thank god you're okay! I was so worried!" She pulled back to punch my shoulder, hard. "Don't you ever scare me like that again! I thought you were dead in a ditch somewhere!"

"I'm sorry," I said, tucking my head.

"Twelve hours without a word!" She was pacing now, her cardigan swirling around her like agitated wings. "After what happened with the Madam, and then you just disappear? I thought they'd gotten to you! I thought—" She stopped, fixing me with a piercing look.

"I'm sorry," I breathed. "Really sorry." I swallowed hard, looking down at my hands. "I ended up...incapaci tated."

She studied me for a long moment, then her shoulders dropped. "You scared me." Her voice was gentler now. "I know you can handle yourself, but after seeing those bruises..." She shook her head. "Just...send a text next time? Even if it's just 'not dead in a ditch' or somethin'?"

"I will. I promise." I met her eyes, trying to convey how much I meant it. "You're the closest thing to family I've got right now."

Twyla's expression softened. She pulled me into another hug, gentler this time. When she pulled back, her entire demeanor had shifted, that familiar mischievous glint returning to her eyes. She hopped onto her desk, scattering a pile of invoices, and grinned. "Okay, now that that's settled—out with it. How was he?"

"I don't know what you mean," I muttered, studying a very interesting spot on the wall where she'd pinned up inspiration photos for her next window display. Most involved constellations and star charts.

"Oh please," she grinned, kicking her feet like an excited child. "Those marks peeking out of your turtleneck paint quite a picture. A biter, huh? And don't think I didn't notice you wincin' every time you sat down." She said, wiggling her brows. If she kept that up, they were going to fly clean off her face.

Heat crept up my neck as I backed toward the door. "I have inventory to finish." I lied. I just needed to get away from her questions. When she'd gotten so invested in my dates? I needed to quash her enthusiasm.

"You can't hide in there forever!" Her giggle chased after me. "Was he as good as he looks—"

I escaped to my apartment, mind spinning with too many thoughts. The door closed with a satisfying click as I turned both locks and the chain, going through the motions that usually made me feel safe. My shoulders dropped as I finally let myself exhale.

"You're late." The wry voice behind me made my heart flutter. "I was starting to think you were avoiding me. I'm hurt."

I spun around, tripping over my own feet. Kronos lounged on my bed like he belonged there, his colossal frame making my twin mattress look absurdly small. One of my books rested open in his hands, and my stomach dropped when I recognized which one—An Ember of Darkness: Beyond the Veil Chronicles, a depraved dark high fantasy romance, the corners of certain pages worn from repeated reading. He looked perfectly at ease, as if breaking into someone's apartment was a casual after-noon activity.

"You have a thing for trauma," he mused, turning another page with deliberate slowness. His silver eyes flicked up to mine, and that wolfish grin spread across his face. He tapped the dog-eared page. "Though after last night, I can see why you've revisited this moment so often. The way the protagonist begs for him to—" He read aloud.

"Get. Out." I meant it to sound commanding, but my voice wavered traitorously. "How did you get in?"

"Your window security is tragic." He didn't look up from the book, still smirking at whatever scene he'd found. "Really, you should invest in better locks. Anyone could just..." He made a casual climbing motion with his free hand, "Climb right in."

I crossed the room in three strides and snatched the book. His hand shot out, catching my wrist with impossible speed. The world tilted as he pulled me off balance, and suddenly I was straddling his lap, our faces inches apart. The book thumped onto the mattress as he pinned my hand by his hip. His other hand caught mine, pressing it flat against his chest where I could feel his heart beating steady and strong.

"We need to talk about last night," he said, all traces of teasing gone from his voice. The sudden shift in his tone made my stomach flip. *Here we go.*

"There's nothing to talk about," I snapped, trying to jerk away. His hold remained immovable, like trying to break free from a steel trap. I focused my glamour, letting it build that magnetic pull that made humans want to please me, protect me, give me anything I asked for. The power hummed under my skin, but Kronos's expression didn't change. I focused my intent and said, "Why don't you let me go, hmm? Could you do that for me, lover?" I tried to smolder and bat my lashes, but playing into it usually increased the effectiveness of my magic.

His lips curved into an amused smirk. "Cute trick." His thumb traced circles on my trapped wrist, sending unwanted shivers down my spine. "But that won't work on me."

"Why the hell not?" The words came out sharper than I intended, fear and frustration making my voice crack. I was tired of being the weakest person in the room.

"Because I'm hot?" His voice rumbled through his chest under my palm. Simple, and entirely unsatisfying.

"If you can't be serious, get out of my apartment." I tried again to pull away, but the attempt just made me more aware of how easily he held me in place.

He pulled me closer until our lips nearly touched, his hand sliding to the small of my back. "I'm a Primal." The words vibrated through his chest under my palm. "All the instincts of my ancestors, none of the mess of shifting. Just pure…" his teeth grazed my lower lip, "predatory drive. Paltry pixie magic doesn't affect me."

I knew what Primals were—lycanthropes diluted through generations of breeding with humans. All the strength, the hunting instincts, the dominance, without the full moon madness. It explained so much—the impossible strength, the way he'd tracked me through the city, why my glamour slid off him like water.

"I wanted to make sure you weren't experiencing any negative effects from last night," he murmured against my jaw. His stubble scraped deliciously against my skin. "The comedown can be intense sometimes. Needed to check that you were okay with everything we did."

"I—" His mouth found that spot behind my ear that made thinking difficult. "I was fine. Just…wasn't what I expected. And I'm not a pixie."

His free hand slid up my back under my sweater, steadying me as he shifted beneath me. "We should establish some boundaries," he said, voice low and rich. "Set a safe word for next time."

"Like not breaking into my home?"

"I'd hardly call that breaking in. The wind could have opened that latch."

I did a double take when I realized what he'd said, "Next time?" I tried to sound skeptical, but my body betrayed me, responding to his proximity. The heat of his palm against my bare skin sent shivers down my spine. "Pretty presumptuous of you."

He hummed against my neck, the sound more growl than laugh. "Is it?" His teeth grazed my throat through the turtleneck. "Choose a word, bunny. Something you'd never say in the heat of the moment."

I swallowed hard, trying to focus despite the way his thumb was now tracing patterns on my hip, each touch making my skin tingle. "Marshmallow."

He pulled back, amusement dancing in those silver eyes. The sudden space between us made it marginally easier to think. "Excuse me?"

"I hate the texture," I muttered, heat creeping up my neck at how ridiculous it sounded. "They're disgusting. All...spongy and powdery, and weird."

"Mmm." He closed the distance again. "I could think of a few ways to change your mind about that." His hand slid lower to the clasp of my pants, following the trail of marks he'd left last night. "But for now...tell me how you're feeling after everything."

"I told you, I'm fine." My words cut off in a gasp as he ground his hips up against me, the movement deliberate and devastating. The tug on my hair at the nape of my neck elicited an embarrassing squeak. Between us, small blue wisps appeared, floating lazily like underwater fireflies. I hadn't meant to release them—these unconscious displays of my power only happened when I was overwhelmed. Kronos didn't comment, but his eyes darkened at the sight, pupils expanding as he watched the lights dance across my skin.

"The truth, Alex." His voice carried that note of command that made my insides turn to liquid. "Were you okay with everything we did?"

"Yes," I managed, trying to gather my scattered thoughts as his fingers traced over sensitive skin. "It was intense, but...good intense. Different." I couldn't look at him. My mind was running away to avoid how intensely he was examining me.

His hand moved to cup my jaw, thumb brushing my lower lip. "And this morning? Why'd you run away like that?"

"I don't do mornings after," I said, though it was getting harder to focus with the way he kept shifting beneath me. "It's not—I just don't."

"Clearly." His teeth caught my earlobe. "Though I had plans for this morning. Breakfast. Maybe..." His hand slid lower to trace the length of me that had stiffened under his coaxing. "But since you climbed out my window..."

Suddenly he was standing, depositing me on shaky legs beside the bed. The loss of contact left me reeling, cold air rushing into the space where his heat had been.

"Sweet dreams, little bunny." *Why does he keep calling me that?* He bent to brush a devastating kiss across my lips. "Consider this payback for leaving me to wake up alone."

"Bunny?" I scoffed. If anything, I was a sly fox. The front door clicked shut behind him and within minutes, the rumble of a motorcycle engine drew me to the window just in time to see him snap his helmet visor closed. He caught my eye, offered a two-finger salute, and roared off into the night.

Chapter Eight

GILDED

The sun was peeking through the slats of my ancient blinds when my phone buzzed across the nightstand. I fumbled for it, still half-asleep, and squinted at the screen.

Kronos: *Be ready at 7. Dress formally.*

My stomach did that annoying flip it had taken to doing whenever his name appeared on my screen. Three weeks of whatever this was between us—dinners at restaurants I couldn't pronounce the names of, nights at his place that left me walking funny the next day, mornings where I'd slip out before he woke—and I still hadn't figured out what we were doing.

I dropped the phone on my chest and stared at the ceiling, watching the shadow of a tree branch dance across the water stain in the corner. The shape reminded me of the way his hair looked spread across his pillow after I'd run my fingers through it. I was getting way too deep into this.

The vibration against my sternum made me jump.

Kronos: *Don't even think about ghosting. I'll hunt you down again.*

I could almost hear the growl in his voice, and my body responded traitorously to the memory of his 'hunt.' Even his texts carried that air of command that somehow bypassed my brain and went straight to my nerves. I'd started Pavlovian-responding to the specific ping I'd set for his messages.

I tapped out a response—*Formal as in a tux or formal as in not jeans?*—and immediately regretted asking. The three dots appeared, disappeared.

Kronos: *You'll find what you need at the store. Twyla's helping.*

I groaned, dropping the phone on my face by accident. Of course, he'd enlisted Twyla. The two of them had struck up an unlikely friendship after he'd shown up at the shop with a vintage brass and crystal barometer for her collection. Now they texted about weather systems and antiques while I pretended not to be jealous of their easy rapport.

I dragged myself out of bed and into the bathroom, where my reflection looked like exactly what I was—someone who'd been up until 3 AM working on a custom order. Dark circles under my eyes, stubble past the 'artfully scruffy' stage and straight into wilderness man territory. I splashed cold water on my face and tried to tame my hair into something that didn't resemble a bird's nest.

"ALEX!" Twyla's voice carried up the stairs, followed by rapid footsteps. "You better be decent because I'm coming in!" My apartment door banged open, and moments later, Twyla burst into the bathroom, nearly giving me a heart attack. She was vibrating with excitement, her bright yellow cardigan clashing gloriously with her purple hair. Today she'd twisted her micro braids into an elaborate updo anchored with what looked like tiny brass bees.

"Why aren't you dressed yet? We have so much to do!" She hopped on the edge of the tub, swinging her feet. "Kronos said you'd be difficult, but honestly, it's almost noon."

I raised an eyebrow at her. "It's 8:30, and I just woke up."

"Semantics." She waved dismissively. "Anyway, your thing is downstairs, and we need to make sure it fits before the alterations lady leaves at three, and then we have to do something about..." she gestured at my face, "all of this."

"What's downstairs? And what's wrong with my face?" I dragged a hand through my damp hair, smoothing it back from my forehead. My skin was clear except for the stubble. I thought I looked good.

"Your tux, obviously. Nothing's wrong with your face—it's one of your better features." She grinned. "Just needs a little maintenance."

"My *what?*"

"Your tuxedo." She enunciated each syllable like I was a slow child. "The one Kronos ordered for tonight's gala."

My stomach dropped. "Gala? What gala? He just said formal."

Twyla's eyes widened. "He didn't tell you? The Winter Solstice Gala at the Metropolitan Museum downtown. It's like *the* event of the season." Her voice dropped to a dramatic whisper. "I heard tickets start at ten thousand dollars *per person.*"

My knees felt weak, and I sat heavily on the closed toilet lid. "Ten *thousand?*" The number made my head spin—that was over six months' rent on my apartment. "That's—he can't expect me to—There's no way I could ever pay him back for something that expensive." I shook my head, trying to clear it. "I can't go to something like that."

"Why not?" Twyla crossed her arms, her excitement giving way to concern. "You've been seeing him for weeks now."

"We're not *seeing* each other," I corrected. "We're just..." What, exactly? Fucking? That didn't seem to cover the dinners, the way he'd pamper me after he did filthy things to me, how he'd read to me from whatever book he was into that week while I dozed against his chest. "It's complicated."

"Uh-huh." She didn't look convinced. "Well, complicated or not, there's a twenty-thousand-dollar custom Armani tux downstairs with your name on it, and a very intimidating woman with pins waiting to make sure it fits your butt perfectly."

I choked on my toothbrush and definitely swallowed some toothpaste. "Twenty thousand—? Absolutely not. That's insane."

"Too late. He already paid for it." She grabbed my hand, tugging me toward the door. "Come on, you can freak out while Madam Beaufort sticks pins dangerously close to your important bits."

Resistance was futile. I ended up letting her drag me downstairs to the back room of the shop, which had been transformed into an impromptu tailor's studio. A rail had been installed along one wall, from which hung the most intimidating piece of clothing I'd ever seen—midnight blue velvet so dark it was almost black, with subtle satin lapels and what appeared to be actual silver buttons.

A severe-looking woman with steel-gray hair pulled into a tight bun stood beside it, tape measure around her neck like a snake. She looked me up and down with the clinical detachment of a butcher assessing a cut of meat.

"Zis is him?" Her French accent was so thick I half-suspected it was put on. She circled me, clicking her tongue. "He is more muscular zan Monsieur Orestes described. Ze shoulders will need adjusting."

"I'm standing right here," I muttered, which earned me a sharp tap on the shoulder with her measuring tape.

"Stand straight," she commanded. "Arms out."

The next hour was a blur of being prodded, measured, and pinned within an inch of my life, all while Twyla flitted around, offering unhelpful commentary and sneaking photos 'for posterity.' By the time Madam Beaufort declared herself satisfied "Ze shoulders are still problematic, but we do what we can with ze time," I felt like I'd been through some bizarre form of torture. Like a butterfly struggling against its wings being pinned by a sadistic nine-year-old.

"This is ridiculous," I hissed once the tailor had retreated to her corner with pins in her mouth, making swift alterations to the jacket. "I can't accept this. And I can't go to some...some high society gala where everything costs more than I make in ten years."

Twyla sat beside me, nudging my shoulder with hers. "Why not?"

"Because I don't belong there!" I gestured helplessly. "I work in a trinket shop. I make leather wallets, for fuck's sake."

"You make *art*. Also, watch it. I own that trinket shop," she corrected. "And you belong wherever you want to be."

I snorted. "Yeah, tell that to the society pages when they ask who I am."

"So, what would you say?" She tilted her head. "If someone asked?"

I looked away, unable to meet her earnest gaze. "I'm no one special."

"That's bullshit, and you know it." Her hand found mine, squeezing it tightly. "You're Alejandro Emiliano Ignacio-Vasquez, a brilliant leatherworker and my best friend. If that's not enough for those stuck-up jack-holes, they can kiss your perfectly tailored butt."

Despite myself, I laughed. "You're always blowing smoke up my ass."

"I'm honest," she countered with a grin. "Now, are you going to text your smoking hot boyfriend and tell him you're backing out, or do you need me to kick your butt into gear?"

"He's not my boyfriend," I sighed, running a hand through my hair. "Fine. I'll tell him myself."

I pulled out my phone, staring at the blank message field. What was I even supposed to say? 'Thanks for the twenty-thousand-dollar tux, but I'm too much of a screwup to be seen with you in public'? 'I'd rather keep this thing between us in the midnight hours where it belongs'?

Before I could type anything, a new message from him appeared.

Kronos: Car will pick you up at 6:45. Looking forward to showing you off tonight.

My throat tightened. Showing me off. Like I was some kind of prize pony. Or worse, like I was one of his possessions, to be displayed when it suited him. The familiar panicky feeling clawed its way up from my stomach.

"I need some air," I mumbled, pushing past Twyla and heading for the back door. I heard her call after me, but I was already outside, gulping down the frigid January air like I was drowning.

The alley behind the shop was quiet, the world muffled by the snow that had fallen in fat, lazy flakes. I leaned against the cold brick, trying to get my breathing under control. This was too much. He kept pushing past the careful boundaries I'd set up. He was getting too close, digging too deep, and eventually he was going to see the truth: that I wasn't worth any of this.

I slid down the wall until I was sitting on the cold ground, snow soaking through my jeans. My breath fogged in front of me as memories flooded back—my father's voice, cold and dismissive: *"You'll never amount to anything, Alejandro. Why can't you be more like your sister?"* I'd been twelve when Penelope's powers had first manifested—dazzling illusions that had transformed our living room into a kaleidoscope of color and light. My gift—that insidious charm that made people want to please me and occasional bursts of light—had seemed pathetic in comparison.

They'd all but forgotten I existed after that. Penelope got the attention, the praise, the special training sessions. I got the leftovers—hand-me-down clothes, cold dinners, disappointed glances. By the time I turned eighteen, the message was clear: I wasn't worth the space I occupied in their home. My father hadn't even looked up from his newspaper when he'd told me to be out by morning. Mother had done nothing to stop it, though I'd heard her crying in her room as I packed my bags.

Two years on the streets had taught me how little my charm was worth when I couldn't afford to keep myself clean, couldn't manage that smile that made humans want to help me. Then Michelle had found me huddled in an alley outside a restaurant that handed out leftovers to the homeless. She'd seen potential where my parents had seen only failure.

"You're too pretty to waste," she'd told me, offering me a job tending bar. At first, it felt like salvation. A warm place to sleep, a steady income, and people who looked at me like I mattered. Until the night she'd caught me using my charm on a customer for extra tips. I thought I'd be fired for sure.

"You've been hidin' things from me, darlin'," she'd purred, her fingers digging into my arm. *"That gift of yours is too valuable to waste behind the bar."*

I didn't know what she meant at first. It didn't click for me until I was on my knees for a sweaty CEO who'd whispered another man's name as he finished. The first time I'd been the dirty secret, the shameful indulgence. I'd been good at it. I'd learned to read what they wanted before they even knew, and shaped myself into their perfect fantasy.

Kronos could dress me up in all the expensive tuxedos in the world, but it wouldn't change what I was. Who I was. The snow fell harder now, melting against my feverish skin, but I barely felt it through the cold emptiness spreading through my chest.

I wasn't the kind of person Kronos needed in his life. I was the fuck up who'd ruined every good thing that came his way, because that's what my father had always said I'd do. He'd been right. Eventually Kronos would see it…and he'd leave me too.

My phone vibrated in my hand. Another message from Kronos.

Kronos: *Should I be concerned about the panic attack Twyla tells me you're having in the alley?*

I scowled, typing back furiously.

Alex: *Tell your spy to mind her own business.*

The reply was immediate.

Kronos: *She's worried about you. So am I.*
Alex: *I'm fine.*

I watched the three dots appear, disappear, then reappear.

Kronos: *If it's too much, we can do something else.*

The reasonable response just made me angrier. I didn't want him to be understanding. I wanted him to be the asshole I could walk away from without a second thought.

Alex: *It's not the gala. It's all of it. The tux, the car, the tickets. I'm not your charity case.*

There was a long pause before his response came through.

Kronos: *Is that what you think this is?*
Alex: *What else would it be? You know who I am.*

My hands were shaking now, and not just from the cold. I was pushing him away on purpose, throwing up walls before he could see how broken I really was. Before he decided I wasn't worth the trouble after all. This way, I got to control when he left me.

Kronos: *I know who you are, Alex. That's why I want you with me tonight. As my date.*

Date. Not hookup, not fuck buddy, not whatever casual arrangement I'd been pretending this was. He wanted more than I was capable of giving him.

Alex: *I can't do this.*

I didn't wait for his response. I shoved my phone deep into my pocket and started walking, needing to put distance between myself and everything. The snow was falling harder now, sticking to my hair and eyelashes, but I barely noticed.

I'd made it about three blocks when I heard the distinctive rumble of his motorcycle. Of course, he wouldn't let me just walk away. That wasn't his style.

The sleek black bike pulled up alongside me, its rider cutting an intimidating figure in dark leather. Kronos pushed up his visor, those silver eyes finding mine.

"Get on the bike, Alex." His voice was calm, but I could hear the tension underneath.

"No." I kept walking, refusing to look at him.

He revved the engine, keeping pace with me. "You're going to freeze to death out here."

"I'm fine."

"You're wearing a t-shirt in winter."

I hadn't even noticed, but he was right. In my rush to get out of the shop, I hadn't grabbed a coat. I was already shivering, my arms covered in goosebumps, but admitting that felt like surrender.

"Go away, Kronos."

He sighed, a plume of white breath disappearing into the falling snow. "Not going to happen. Either get on the bike, or I'll throw you over my shoulder and put you on it."

I stopped walking, finally turning to glare at him. "Why can't you just leave me alone? I told you I can't do this."

"You said you can't do 'this'," he replied, cutting the engine and swinging his leg over the bike. Even in the swirling snow, his movements were fluid, predatory. *Gods, how is he always so fucking perfect! It's not fair.* "You never explained what 'this' is."

"This!" I gestured between us. "Whatever fantasy you've built up in your head about me. I'm not some—some trophy you can dress up and parade around at your fancy parties."

He took a step closer, his face unreadable. "Is that what you think I'm doing?"

"What else would it be?" I wrapped my arms around myself, trying to stop shivering. "You buy me expensive clothes, take me to places I could never afford, like I'm some kind of—pet. Hell, you even call me your *pet* and bunny. Docile and helpless and in need of your fucking rescue."

"That's not—" He ran a hand through his hair, leaving it standing up in damp spikes. "That's not what this is. You're being ridiculous."

"Then what is it?" My voice cracked. "Because from where I'm standing, it looks a lot like you trying to *fix* me."

Something flickered across his face—hurt, maybe, or frustration. "I don't want to fix you, Alex. There's nothing to fix."

I was too angry to hold it back anymore. "Right. Because I'm so perfectly well-adjusted. Like I'm not some trussed up whore. Like you won't ride off on your stupid bike and find some other fuck up. The entire state knows what I am, especially the men that'd be at this fucking Gala."

"And what's that?" He closed the distance between us, his heat radiating even through his riding jacket. "What do you think you are?"

"Damaged goods." Worthless. Stupid. The words tasted sour on my tongue. I swallowed hard. "I was the guy businessmen slipped away to see when they told their partners they were 'working late.'" My voice cracked. "I'm not the kind they take on fancy dates. I'm the kind they pretend never existed in the morning."

His hand shot out, catching my wrist before I could back away. "Don't." His voice was low, dangerous. "Don't talk about yourself like that."

"Why not? It's the truth." I tried to pull away, but his grip was unyielding. "I've spent years performing for clients. I'm good at making people feel special, making them think they matter for an hour or an evening. It's what I do best."

"Is that what you think you've been doing with me?" He clutched his helmet in his hands so tightly I thought it might shatter. "Performing?"

"I—" The words died in my throat. Because that was the problem, wasn't it? I hadn't been performing with him. With him, I'd been terrifyingly, vulnerably real. "I don't know how to be anything else," I whispered finally.

His expression softened, and he tugged me closer, out of the falling snow and into the shelter of a nearby storefront. "Alex." Just my name, but he said it like it meant something. Like I meant something.

"I can't go," I mumbled. "I can't stand in a room full of important people pretending I belong there."

"You would belong there." His thumb traced gentle circles on the inside of my wrist, his touch warming my cold skin. "But if it makes you that uncomfortable, we won't go."

I blinked, certain I'd misheard. "What?"

"We won't go," he repeated. "I'll tell them we can't make it."

"But the tickets—"

"It's just money." He shrugged as if ten thousand dollars was pocket change. To him, maybe it was. "I bought them because I wanted to spend the evening with you, and I thought you might enjoy the music and art. I'm realizing now that I should have asked you first."

The fight drained out of me all at once, leaving me exhausted and cold. "I don't understand you."

"What's to understand?" His voice was gentle now, the storm draining from his features. "I like you. I want to be with you. It doesn't matter where."

"It's not that simple."

"It could be." He reached up, brushing snow from my hair with a gentleness that made my chest ache. "If you'd stop running away every time things get real."

I didn't have an answer for that, because he was right. I'd been running—from him, from the possibility of something genuine, from the terrifying prospect that I might deserve more than what I'd settled for. There was no way I could admit that to him, though.

"I'm freezing," I said instead, a weak deflection that he saw right through.

He sighed, shrugging out of his riding jacket. "Here."

"No."

"Just take the damn jacket, Alex." He draped it over my shoulders, the leather still warm from his body. It smelled like him. "Before I have to explain to Twyla why I let you freeze to death."

The weight of it settled around me, heavy and comforting. I slipped my arms into the sleeves, instantly enveloped in warmth that had nothing to do with the leather and everything to do with the man standing before me.

"What do you want from me?" I asked the question, stripped of its earlier accusation.

He stepped closer, crowding me against the storefront. One hand came up to cup my jaw, his palm warm against my cold cheek. "Everything you're willing to give," he said. "But only what you want to."

"What if that's nothing?" I challenged, even as I leaned into his touch like a flower seeking the sun.

His lips quirked up in a ghost of that wolfish smile that never failed to make my heart race. "Then I'll respect that. After I do everything in my power to change your mind."

I should have pushed him away then, should have stuck to my plan to keep this—whatever it was—casual and uncomplicated. Instead, I reached for him, my hands fisting in his sweater, pulling him closer until I could bury my face in the crook of his neck.

"I'm sorry," I murmured against his skin.

His arms wound around me like he was afraid to let go. "Nothing to be sorry for." His voice rumbled through his chest and into mine where we pressed together. "Though I still think it's a shame the world won't get to see you in that tux. You looked devastating in the fitting."

I pulled back, narrowing my eyes at him. "How would you know? You weren't there."

His grin turned mischievous. "Twyla sent pictures."

"Of course she did." I shook my head, trying and failing to hold on to my irritation. "You two are a menace together."

"She cares about you." His expression grew serious again. "So do I."

Those three simple words hung between us, loaded with meaning I wasn't ready to unpack. I looked away, focusing on the snow collecting on the sidewalk, the way it muffled the sounds of the city.

"So what now?" I asked.

"Now?" He stepped back, giving me space I wasn't sure I wanted. "Now we get you somewhere warm before you turn into an icicle. And then…" He tilted his head, considering. "And then we figure out what you want to do tonight."

"Like what?"

"Whatever you want." He gestured to his bike. "We could grab dinner somewhere comfortable. Or go back to my place—just to talk," he added quickly, seeing my expression. "Or I can take you home, if that's what you need."

The offer of choice was so simple, yet it left me speechless. When was the last time someone had asked what I wanted without an agenda?

I took a deep breath, the cold air stinging my lungs. Something in me was shifting, walls crumbling that I wasn't ready to let fall completely. "I can't do dinner. Not tonight."

His expression didn't change, but I caught the slight tightening around his eyes. "Alright."

"I need..." I ran a hand through my snow-damp hair, searching for words that wouldn't hurt him but would still protect me. "I need some space. To figure things out."

"Space," he repeated, the word neutral in a way that told me he was carefully controlling his reaction. "How much space are we talking about here?"

"I don't know." That was true. I didn't know what I needed, only that the intensity of whatever was happening between us felt like drowning. "A few days, maybe. I'm not—" I looked up at him, needing him to understand. "I'm not ending this. I just need to get my head straight."

He studied me for a long moment, his silver eyes unreadable in the fading light. Then he nodded once, decisive. "Take whatever time you need."

"You're not mad?"

A wry smile touched his lips. "I didn't say that, but I understand needing time to process." He reached out, brushing snowflakes from my shoulder with a gentleness that made my chest ache. "Just don't disappear on me."

"I won't," I promised, meaning it despite the fear still coiled in my stomach.

He swung a leg over his bike, the engine roaring to life with a turn of his key. "Do you want a ride home?"

I shook my head. "I think I'll walk. Clear my head."

"It's freezing."

"I have your jacket," I reminded him, pulling it tighter around me.

He looked like he wanted to argue, but he just nodded again. "Keep it. It looks better on you, anyway."

Before I could respond, he lowered his visor and pulled away from the curb, snow swirling in his wake. I watched until his taillights disappeared around a corner, feeling both relieved and strangely bereft.

The walk back to the shop was quiet, the snow muffling the usual city sounds. I used the time to sort through the tangle of emotions Kronos had stirred up—the fear, the want, the lingering certainty that I'd find some way to ruin this, too.

By the time I reached Twyla's, my fingers were numb and my thoughts were still chaotic, but one thing had become clear: whatever this thing with Kronos was, I wasn't ready to let it go. Not yet.

His leather jacket hung heavy on my shoulders as I climbed the stairs to my apartment, carrying his scent, his warmth. A reminder that, for now at least, I had been given a choice—and the space to figure out what I wanted.

I just hoped I wouldn't take too long to figure it out.

Chapter Nine

THE HEIST

The sequined bodysuit itched in places I didn't want to think about. I tugged at the tight fabric, trying to find a comfortable position as I crouched behind the dumpster, watching the back door of Ogygia. My heart hammered so hard I was certain anyone passing by would hear it.

It hadn't been that long since I'd walked out of this place, and now I was going back in. But Kronos was out-of-town tracking his bail jumper, Twyla was visiting her parents for the weekend, and the timing couldn't be more perfect. The Madam always had her weekly meeting with her higher-ups on Thursday nights—the one night I could be certain she wouldn't be here.

More importantly, tonight was my last chance. I'd almost deleted Cassie's mass text without reading it—seeing her name still brought back too many memories. But the subject line caught my eye.

Cassie: *WTF contracts moving???*

Her message had gone out to everyone who'd ever worked at Ogygia.

Cassie: *OMG guys! Just overheard Madam telling Granite they're moving ALL performer contracts to some offsite vault tomorrow! Like a bank security box that only SHE can access! Why would she do that??*

Cassie hadn't meant to give me a deadline, but she had. Once those contracts left the premises, I'd never get mine back. Seven years of magical servitude would become my inescapable reality. I couldn't let that happen.

The back door opened, spilling neon light and thumping bass into the alley. Two dancers stumbled out, laughing as they lit cigarettes. The blue-skinned nymph was new, but I recognized Rio—his iridescent scales catching the light as he exhaled a cloud of smoke.

I shrank deeper into the shadows, waiting for my moment. The familiar scent of clove cigarettes mixed with the alley's garbage stench sent me spiraling into memories I'd tried to bury—hungry hands grabbing at me as I danced, the Madam's lotus-eater magic making the air syrupy, the weight of eyes watching through hidden cameras.

Rio flicked his cigarette into a puddle. "Break's over. Maddy will have our asses if we're late for the nine o'clock rush."

The door clicked shut behind them. I counted to thirty, then moved, keeping low and fast. The keypad lock hadn't changed—still the same code as when I worked here. 0-6-6-6, the Madam's twisted idea of a joke. The door beeped softly and unlocked.

The service corridor was exactly as I remembered—dingy emergency lights casting everything in sickly yellow, walls vibrating with bass from the main floor. My glamour was already working, a subtle push that made eyes slide past me, minds dismissing me as unimportant. It wouldn't hold against direct scrutiny, but it was enough to get me through the back halls unnoticed.

The dancers' dressing room lay just ahead—the only path to the Madam's office that wouldn't take me through the main floor. I slipped inside, hit by the familiar chaos of the pre-show rush. Costumes hung from every available surface, makeup cluttered vanities, and glitter seemed to coat everything like a fine, sparkly dust. I ducked my head, moving toward the far corner where a hidden door connected to the Madam's private quarters.

"Oh my GOD! ALEX?"

I froze, heart stopping as the voice rang out across the room. The glamour only worked if people weren't looking for you, and clearly, I'd been recognized. I turned to find Dario staring at me, mouth open in shock. His neon yellow body paint glowed under the vanity lights, matching his platform boots and the tiny shorts that left little to the imagination.

"Shh!" I hissed, darting over to him before he could call more attention to me. "Keep it down, *por favor.*"

"You're ALIVE!" Dario whispered, pulling me into a bone-crushing hug that left me covered in his body paint. "We thought you were DEAD or something equally TRAGIC when you just VANISHED one day! Michelle was BESIDE herself, honey! And not in a good way!"

I extricated myself from his grip, trying to wipe the yellow paint off my sequined disguise. "Yeah, well, I had my reasons."

"Clearly!" Dario's eyes widened as he took in my outfit. "Are you BACK? Please tell me you're back! It's been SO BORING without you! The new boys are all TERRIBLE and have NO rhythm whatsoever. I've been stuck dancing with Trevor—TREVOR!—can you IMAGINE?"

I glanced nervously at the door leading to the Madam's office. Every second I spent here increased the risk of getting caught. "No, I'm not coming back. I just... I need to get something I left behind."

Dario tilted his head, eyes narrowing. "Left behind? After all this time? What could be SO important that you'd risk coming back HERE?"

"It's complicated," I said, trying to edge toward the office door. "Look, it was great seeing you, but I really need to—"

"DANCERS!" A voice bellowed from the stage entrance. "Five minutes to places! And someone find Dario—he's on in the opening number!"

Dario grabbed my arm. "Tell me EVERYTHING later! But right now, we're short a dancer because Mikel got food poisoning from that QUESTIONABLE sushi place across the street!" His eyes lit up with an idea that made my stomach drop. "Oh! OH! You should FILL IN! Just like old times!"

"What? No! Dario, I can't—"

"You HAVE to! Otherwise they'll notice something's wrong! Besides, you're already DRESSED for it!" He gestured at my sequined disguise. "And you always were the BEST at the routine!"

Before I could protest further, Dario was dragging me toward the stage, chattering a mile a minute. "It's the SAME routine as before—you remember? The one where we all come out in masks for the first half? NO ONE will know it's you! It's PERFECT!"

Panic clawed up my throat as we neared the wings. The music was already starting—a pulsing, hypnotic beat I remembered all too well. My body responded, muscle memory kicking in despite my mind screaming to run.

"I don't have a mask," I said. "Dario, I can't be seen here—"

"HERE!" He snatched an ornate mask from his vanity—all feathers and jewels, covering the upper half of the face. "It's for the SECOND act, but you can borrow it!"

The mask settled over my face, surprisingly comfortable. Through the eyeholes, I saw dancers lining up, preparing to enter. My feet moved without conscious decision, taking their place in line. *What am I doing? This is insane. I should be running in the opposite direction.*

But there was no time to escape now. Dario gave me a little push as the music swelled, and then I was onstage, blinded by spotlights, surrounded by dancers moving in perfect synchronicity. My body took over, remembering steps I thought I'd forgotten. The crowd was a faceless mass beyond the lights, their energy washing over me like a physical force.

For one terrifying, exhilarating moment, I was back—Will-o'-Wisp, the Madam's star attraction, the dancer who could make anyone fall in love for the right price. The music pulsed through me, my arms extended, body rolling in practiced waves that drew appreciative shouts from the audience. The sequins caught the light, throwing prisms across the stage as I moved.

I glimpsed Granite by the main entrance, his crystalline skin unmistakable even in the shifting lights. His gaze swept the stage, lingering on me longer than comfort allowed. Did he recognize me despite the mask? I turned away, focusing on the routine, letting the dance carry me across the stage and closer to the wings.

As soon as we hit the final pose and the lights dimmed for the next number, I slipped backstage, gasping for breath. Adrenaline coursed through my veins, making my hands shake as I tore off the mask. *I'm more out of shape than I realized.*

"You were MAGNIFICENT!" Dario gushed, appearing beside me in a cloud of glitter. "The crowd LOVED you!"

"I have to go," I said, already backing toward the dressing rooms. "Thanks for the cover, but I need to—"

"Oh, GO do your mysterious WHATEVER it is," he waved. "But you OWE me! I'll cover for you if anyone asks—I'll say you got SICK or something!"

I squeezed his arm in gratitude before darting back to the dressing rooms, now empty with everyone either performing or preparing for their next number. The door to the Madam's office was unguarded—exactly as I'd hoped. Her security system relied more on magical wards than physical locks, but those were calibrated to stop intruders from entering the club, not former employees moving within it.

The office was opulent, dripping with the Madam's particular brand of new-money garishness—velvet and gilt and crystal chandeliers. Behind her massive desk, a portrait of herself gazed down with cold, predatory eyes. Even painted, they seemed to follow me as I crossed the plush carpet.

The safe was hidden behind the portrait—because of course it was, subtlety had never been her strong suit. I swung the frame aside, revealing the sleek metal door with its digital keypad. I hesitated, mind racing through possible combinations. Her birthday? No, she changed it depending on her mood. The club's founding date? Possibly, but I'd never known the actual date.

Then I remembered overhearing her on the phone once, drunkenly shouting at someone about "the day it all began"—May 19, 1973. Worth a shot.

I punched in 051973, holding my breath.

The pad flashed red. Incorrect.

I tried again, reversing it: 731905.

Another red flash. Two more attempts before it would lock me out.

Think, Alex. What would a narcissistic lotus-eater choose as her code?

My eyes drifted to the portrait, to the Madam's self-satisfied smile. Of course. I entered 060666—the same as the back door code. Her favorite number repeated, because why wouldn't she use the same code twice? Security had never been her concern; fear kept people in line, not locks.

The pad flashed green. The safe door swung open with an expensive whisper of well-oiled hinges.

Inside, neatly organized folders lined the interior, each labeled with names—her collection of souls, contracts, and blackmail. My hands shook as I flipped through them, leaving smudges of yellow paint on the edges. Martinez... Miller... Nguyen...

There. Vasquez, Alejandro E.

I pulled out the folder, my pulse thundering in my ears. Inside was the contract I'd signed when I'd been at my lowest point, written on what I now recognized was human skin, the ink shimmering with a sickly green glow. My signature at the bottom stood out in dried blood—my blood, taken the night she'd "rescued" me from the streets.

Nausea surged through me as I stared at the document that had held me captive for so long. Seven years of service, it stipulated, with provisions for "visual recording and distribution of performances both public and private." No wonder she'd fought so hard to keep me—I was worth a fortune to her in streaming revenue alone.

I folded the contract, tucking it into the slim pocket hidden in my disguise. My hands left yellow smears on the safe's interior as I closed it, the portrait swinging back into place with a soft thud.

I'd done it. I actually had my contract.

A scraping sound from the outer office froze me in place. Someone was coming. I darted behind the door just as it swung open, pressing myself into the shadow of a massive bookcase.

"I swear I saw someone come in here," came a gravelly voice—Granite.

"You're paranoid," replied a second voice, the wispy tenor of Smokey. "Probably just another of Dario's conquests. He's always sneaking them back here."

"Maybe." Granite didn't sound convinced. His heavy footsteps crossed to the desk. "But the Madam would skin us both if anything happened to her collection."

I held my breath, willing my racing heart to quiet. The contract felt like it was burning against my skin, its magical properties perhaps responding to my fear. A thin bead of sweat trickled down my spine.

"The safe looks undisturbed," Smokey noted. "See? Nothing to worry about."

"What's this?" Granite's voice sharpened. "Paint? On the safe?"

My heart stopped. I'd forgotten about the paint from Dario's hug. I'd left evidence all over the safe.

"Check the files," Granite ordered. "Now."

The sound of the safe reopening made my blood run cold. I needed a distraction, something to get them away from the safe before they noticed which file was missing.

I focused on the chandelier overhead, calling on my will-o'-wisp magic. A thin tendril of blue fire snaked from my fingertips, invisible to the enforcers as it climbed up the wall and across the ceiling. With a thought, I sent it into the crystal fixture, where it danced among the prisms like a stray reflection.

Then I made it explode.

Glass shattered everywhere as the chandelier burst in a spectacular display of blue flame and crystal shrapnel. The enforcers shouted in surprise, ducking for cover.

I bolted from my hiding place, making for the door. In my haste, the contract slipped from my pocket, fluttering to the floor like a dying moth.

"There!" Smokey shouted, darkness flowing from his fingertips. A tendril of shadow snaked around my wrist, burning cold against my skin. I yelped, trying to wrench free as another tendril reached for the fallen contract.

"No!" I couldn't lose it now, not when I was so close. Magic surged through me—not the gentle lights I usually produced, but something wilder, more desperate. Blue fire erupted from my trapped hand, burning through Smokey's darkness like acid through paper. He howled, the shadows recoiling.

I dove for the contract, fingers just grazing the ancient skin as a tendril of shadow wrapped around my wrist. I cried out in pain, my arm jerked backward at an unnatural angle.

"Gotcha," Smokey hissed, darkness crawling up my arm like living frost.

The contract lay on the floor, just inches from my outstretched fingers but impossibly far. Another shadow tendril snaked toward it, gathering the precious document and pulling it back toward the safe.

"No!" I shouted, desperation fueling my magic. Blue fire erupted from my trapped hand, burning through Smokey's darkness. He howled as his shadows recoiled, but it was too late—the contract was already back in the safe's maw, the heavy door swinging shut with a final-sounding click.

"Get him!" Granite growled, crystalline knuckles cracking as he advanced.

I ran, blue wisps trailing from my fingers as I desperately tried to put distance between myself and the enforcers. The corridor outside was chaotic—dancers responding to the crash, security running toward the commotion. I pushed through them, using the confusion to my advantage.

"ALEX! Here!" Dario appeared, gesturing frantically toward a service exit. As I sprinted past, he stuck out his foot, sending a security guard crashing into Granite. Whether it was intentional or just fortunate clumsiness, I didn't stop to ask.

The cool night air hit my face as I burst through the exit, running blindly down the alley. Behind me, I heard shouts and the distinctive sound of Smokey's shadows slithering across concrete.

But I had one advantage. I knew these streets better than they did. Three years of working at Ogygia and their volatile staff had taught me every shortcut, every hiding place within ten blocks. I ducked into a storm drain, crawling through the narrow tunnel until I emerged two streets over.

I didn't stop running until I was certain I'd lost them, collapsing against a brick wall in an unfamiliar part of town.

I'd failed. The contract was still in the Madam's possession, my one chance to free myself completely—gone. But I was alive, and that counted for something. They'd be looking for me now, even more determined than before. I needed somewhere safe, somewhere they wouldn't think to look for me.

My phone buzzed in my pocket, making me jump. A text from Twyla.

Twyla: *Flight canceled!! Stupid weather! Back at the shop. Movie night? Bring pizza if ur around.*

Shit. I couldn't go home now. She'd take one look at me and know where I'd been. Worse, she might think I was trying to go back to work there.

Kronos's brownstone was close. He was out of town, but I had a key—"for emergencies," he'd said with that wolfish grin. This definitely qualified.

The sequined bodysuit chafed as I walked, drawing strange looks from the few people still out at this hour. Yellow paint covered my hands and chest, marking me as clearly as a neon sign. I tapped out a quick reply to Twyla.

Alex: *Out with friends. Don't wait up.*

It wasn't entirely a lie—I had been with people I used to consider friends, in a manner of speaking.

By the time I reached Kronos's place, my feet were blistered and my nerves were shot. The house was dark and silent as I let myself in, immediately feeling safer within these walls. His scent lingered everywhere—cedar and storm and something uniquely him that made my shoulders drop from around my ears.

I headed straight for the shower, peeling off the ruined disguise and stepping under scalding water. Paint swirled down the drain, along with the sweat of fear and the phantom feeling of Smokey's shadows on my skin. I scrubbed until my skin was raw, trying to wash away any trace of Ogygia.

Clean and exhausted, I padded naked to Kronos's bedroom. My wrist still burned where Smokey's shadow had gripped me, a faint dark mark circling the skin like a bruise. So close. I'd been so close to having my freedom in my hands.

His bed was made with military precision, the dark sheets cold without his supernatural warmth. I slipped between them anyway, burying my face in his pillow, breathing in his scent. For the first time since entering Ogygia, my heart rate slowed to something approaching normal.

I hadn't intended to sleep there. The plan had been to shower, destroy all evidence of what I'd done, and return to my apartment above Twyla's shop. But the moment my head hit Kronos's pillow, surrounded by his scent, the adrenaline crash hit hard. My eyes grew heavy, my limbs leaden with exhaustion.

Just a few minutes, I told myself. Just until I stop shaking.

The Madam wouldn't let this go easily. The enforcers would be looking for me now, even more determined than before. But for tonight, wrapped in Kronos's sheets, I allowed myself to feel safe. Tomorrow would bring consequences—they always did. For now, I just needed to breathe.

And plan my next move.

Chapter Ten

MIDNIGHT CRAVING

I stirred my coffee absently, watching steam curl into the winter air through the shop's front window. The ceramic mug warmed my stiff fingers, but it did nothing to ease the tension coiling in my stomach.

Those first few days after our confrontation had been strange—a weird limbo where I'd check my phone, both hoping for and dreading his messages. He'd said that he had to leave town for a bounty, and he didn't know how long he'd be gone. Part of me had been relieved, grateful for the forced distance to sort through my feelings. The other part had started counting the days until he returned.

My phone buzzed again. I knocked over my drink in my rush to check it, earning an annoyed look from the sprite barista wiping down nearby tables. Just a client asking about their order, I'd gotten a little behind. I'd half hoped it was another message like this morning's.

Kronos: *I have plans for you, little bunny. Hope you're ready to play.*

Six hours until midnight. Six hours until I was supposed to climb those imposing brownstone steps again. The last two months had been a special kind of torture—brief calls at odd hours as he tracked his mark across state lines. He'd been vague about the actual bounty, just that it involved someone "making unfortunate choices that endangered our kind."

I checked my phone again. 5:54 PM. Still six hours. The coffee shop's evening crowd buzzed around me, people rushing to finish errands before dark. A woman in an expensive coat ordered some complicated drink with "extra fairy dust," literal sparkles dancing off her cup as she passed my table. Everything felt surreal, dreamlike. Maybe because I hadn't slept in days, too wound up with anticipation.

The past two months had been a blur of long days at the shop and longer nights staring at my phone. Every time it buzzed, my heart would jump, wondering if it was another message from him. Sometimes they were innocent enough—asking about my day, commenting on some bizarre thing he'd seen while tracking his mark. Others left me squirming in my desk chair, having to take breaks from tooling leather because I was too flustered to keep working.

Last night was devastating. A photo of his hotel room's massive bed, followed by a detailed account of what he planned to do to me on a bed that size. I'd had to read it in pieces, each paragraph making it harder to breathe. The memory of it still made heat crawl up my neck.

I took another sip of coffee, grimacing at how bitter it had grown while I'd let it cool. The cup was just something to do with my hands anyway—the last thing I needed was more caffeine when I already felt like I might vibrate out of my skin. Two months without his touch had left me numb and kind of pissy. I had to remember that I'd done this to myself.

Twyla had noticed my distraction, of course. She'd taken to making suggestive comments every time my phone went off at work. "Is that your hunter checking his snares?" she'd ask, waggling her eyebrows until I fled the front counter. At least she'd stopped asking for details after that first morning, though her knowing smirks whenever I adjusted my collar hadn't let up. She'd left me a cold compress and a concealer that matched my skin tone on my bathroom sink. I had to take her key back.

The worst part was how easily he'd slipped past my defenses. One intense night, and suddenly I was counting hours until I could see him again. That wasn't me. I didn't do relationship things, didn't let people get close enough to matter. Somehow Kronos had gotten under my skin, worked his way into my thoughts until I caught myself daydreaming about how he touched me in the aftermath of our encounters.

Even now, my fingers traced the rim of my coffee cup, remembering how his hands felt on my skin. The messages had gotten more intense over the past week as he got closer to catching his mark. Last night he'd called—the first time in days—and just hearing his voice, that accent thick with promise, had nearly undone me.

"Soon, my sweet, darling bunny," he'd growled, and I could picture that predatory smile. "I can't wait to show you what I have planned for us when I get back. Are you sure you're ready?"

Ready. As if I could be ready for whatever he had planned. The last text had mentioned something about rope, testing my limits, and making me beg. Just thinking about it made my pulse quicken. I checked my phone again. 5:58 PM.

The coffee shop had emptied as dusk crept in. Street lamps flickered to life outside, casting strange shadows through Twyla's window displays across the street. I should head home and get some work done instead of sitting here letting my imagination run wild. Lately, my apartment felt too quiet.

I couldn't stop thinking about the risk I'd taken three nights ago. With Kronos out of town and Twyla visiting her parents for the weekend, I'd convinced myself it was the perfect time to try breaking into Madam Michelle's club. Not to dance or drink, but to get to her vault—to find my contract and destroy it once and for all.

The place had been different in the quiet hours before dawn. I'd made it all the way to the office, had even gotten the safe open, my contract in hand—only to trip the magical alarm I hadn't known existed. I'd barely escaped with my life, leaving the contract behind in my rush to flee.

The barista was giving me pointed looks now, her iridescent wings fluttering with impatience as she wiped down the same counter for the third time. Behind her, the 'Open' sign flickered once, twice—a not-so-subtle hint. Outside, the last rays of sunlight painted the sky in shades of blood and gold, casting long shadows across the empty tables. The weather had turned bitter cold again, winter refusing to release its grip on the city despite the calendar insisting it should be warming up.

I shoved my phone in my pocket and reached for my coat, mind still tangled in thoughts of midnight. My elbow caught the edge of my mug, sending it teetering toward disaster. I lunged for it, fingers just grazing the handle before it crashed to the checkered floor. Coffee splashed across the black-and-white tiles, ceramic shards skittering in every direction like startled insects.

"Sorry! I'm so sorry," I stammered, dropping to my knees to gather the larger pieces.

The sprite's wings stilled as she glared down at me, her tiny features pinched with annoyance. "Don't bother," she said, voice like wind chimes in a storm. "Just go. We're closing."

Heat crept up my neck as I fumbled for my wallet, pulling out a twenty and setting it on the nearest clean tile. "For the mug and...the trouble."

She snatched it up with delicate fingers, tucking it into the pocket of her apron with practiced efficiency. "Maybe get a to-go cup next time, hmm?"

Properly chastised, I pulled on my coat and slunk toward the door. The bell chimed as I stepped into the cold, a gust of winter air slapping my heated cheeks. My breath fogged in the air like dragon smoke, curling upward to join the steam from the takeaway cup clutched in my hand—a last-minute purchase from the counter to justify how long I'd been loitering and now my only defense against the biting cold. Music drifted from Ogygia a few blocks away, the bass pulsing as night creatures woke, their shadows stretching across brick walls in anticipation of darkness.

I turned away from the sound, taking the long way home. Six hours. Just six more hours and—

The impact knocked the coffee from my hand, sending it splashing across the sidewalk. I'd walked straight into what felt like a wall, too lost in thoughts of midnight to watch where I was going. Looking up, my stomach dropped to the ground.

The granite-skinned enforcer stood like a statue carved from a nightmare, his crystalline features catching the last light like broken glass. Behind him loomed his partner, the one wreathed in perpetual shadow, darkness coiling around him like smoke.

"Look who tried his luck at being a cat burglar." The words scraped out like gravel over steel. "The Madam's been looking forward to seeing you again."

Granite took one thundering step closer. "Breaking into her private vault. Trying to destroy valuable property." His granite fingers flexed. "She doesn't take kindly to theft, you know."

I backed up, my heart hammering against my ribs. Smokey hadn't spoken yet, but darkness writhed around him like living ink, reaching toward me with smoky tendrils.

"That contract is mine," I said, proud that my voice didn't shake. "I have a right to take it."

"No," Granite took another step forward. Behind him, streetlights began flickering to life, their witch-light casting strange shadows across the hard lines of his frame. "Everything in the Madams club belongs to her. Including you, whether you like it or not."

Ice shot through my veins. They'd been watching for me to resurface, waiting to catch me alone. This would not go well for me.

"The thing is," he continued, closing the distance between us, "the Madam doesn't like it when people try to steal from her. Especially not after she's been so generous."

"That bitch *fucking sold me*." The word slipped out before I could stop it.

His smile was like watching stone crack. "Wrong choice of words."

The first blow caught me in the ribs, right where he'd left bruises the last time I saw him. I stumbled backward, trying to remember how to breathe. Smokey circled around, cutting off my escape route. The street had emptied, everyone else sensing the violence about to unfold.

"She gave you a job when no one else would touch you," Granite spat. "Fed you, clothed you, put a roof over your head. You were her favorite."

"She sold videos of me without my consent," I gasped, tasting copper as I spat blood onto the concrete. "Filmed me without my knowledge. Made money off my body without giving me a single fucking cent."

The kick to my stomach lifted me off the ground. I rolled, trying to get my feet under me, but darkness wrapped around my ankle like a vise. The shadow enforcer dragged me back, his touch burning cold through my jeans.

Panic clawed up my throat. I reached for my glamour, letting it build until it spilled out of me in waves. "Stop," I commanded, putting everything I had into the word. "Let me go."

The shadow's grip loosened for just a moment—long enough for me to wrench free and scramble to my feet. I ran.

Their footsteps thundered behind me as I darted down the nearest alley. A gunshot cracked through the air, brick dust exploding beside my head. *What the fuck? They're trying to kill me!*

The cemetery gates loomed ahead, iron bars casting long shadows in the dying light. I vaulted over the low stone wall instead, my dress shoes slipping on frost-covered grass. Another shot rang out, closer this time. My heart threatened to burst from my chest as I weaved between headstones.

A massive marble tomb of some long-dead wealthy family rose before me like salvation. I crashed behind it just as another bullet chipped the corner, sending white dust showering over my shoulders. My lungs burned with each desperate breath, the taste of blood sharp on my tongue.

"Come out, come out, pretty boy," Granite's voice echoed across the graves. "You're just making this worse for yourself."

Footsteps crunched on frozen grass. I pressed myself harder against the cold stone, trying to make myself smaller. The shadow enforcer's darkness was seeping across the ground like fog, searching.

"The Madam might have let you live, before," the voice was closer now. "But after trying to steal from her? Breaking into her personal vault? She'd want me to make an example of you."

I was going to die here. Die hiding behind a stranger's tomb, and no one would ever know what really happened to me. They'd toss my body in an open grave and cover me with a little dirt. No one would be the wiser. Would Kronos wonder why I didn't show up? He'd think I'd ghosted him for good. It'd be in the literal sense and he wouldn't even get the irony.

Heavy boots crossed the grass with deliberate slowness, passing right by my hiding spot. A familiar hand dropped onto my head, and I jumped back with my hands over my head, expecting a crushing blowing that never came.

"Stay down," Kronos's voice was deadly soft. "I'll handle this."

"Run," I hissed, grabbing for his sleeve. "Kronos, they have guns—"

His laugh was dark, primal—nothing like the playful sounds I remembered. The air around him vibrated with barely contained power. When he stepped out from behind the tomb, he prowled toward the sound of the enforcers with no fear.

"Gentlemen." His accent was thicker, rougher. "I believe you're hunting something that belongs to me."

Granite sneered. "This doesn't concern you, stranger. Get out while you still got your kneecaps."

"Is that so?" The temperature seemed to drop as Kronos moved forward. Something dark and ancient rolled off him in waves, making the shadow enforcer's darkness look like child's play. Could he be something else aside from a Primal? I wondered if they ever mixed with non-humans? "See, I just spent two months tracking down a mark who thought he could expose our kind to danger. Messy business. Then, I come home to find two thugs shooting at my partner."

"I said back off, you freak!" Another gunshot cracked through the cemetery. Kronos moved like liquid shadow, the bullet missing him by inches. His smile was all teeth now, sharp and hungry in the growing dark.

"Oh good," he purred, rolling his shoulders. "I was hoping you'd make this interesting."

I could hear Granite's fist connect with solid muscle as Kronos engaged them. The sound of the fight was brutal—sharp cracks of impact, grunts of exertion, the scrape of boots on frozen ground. I peered around the edge of the tomb, unable to stop myself.

Kronos moved like a force of nature. The shadow enforcer's darkness tried to wrap around him, but slid off that supernatural energy rolling from his skin. He caught Granite's next punch, using the enforcer's own momentum to slam him into a headstone. The crack of stone splitting echoed through the cemetery.

"You know what I love about cemeteries?" Kronos's voice carried that deadly amusement as he dodged another swing. "No witnesses." His fist connected with Granite's jaw, the impact sounding like boulders colliding. "No one to hear you scream."

Smokey tried to flank him, tendrils of darkness reaching. Kronos spun impossibly fast, catching him by the throat. "Amateur, who taught you to fight?" he growled, before throwing him into Granite. They went down in a tangle of limbs and cursing.

Another gunshot. This time, I saw Kronos's expression change—something ancient and wild crossing his features as he snarled. The sound made every hair on my body stand on end.

The next few moments were a blur of violence. Kronos moved with impossible speed, each strike precise and devastating. When Granite tried to rise, Kronos caught him with a kick that sent shards scattering across the frost-covered grass. The smokey darkness writhed, trying to engulf Kronos, but that primal energy rolling off him ate through the shadows like acid.

"Here's what's going to happen," Kronos said, his voice carrying that deadly calm that was worse than anger. He had Granite pinned, one knee pressed into the enforcer's chest hard enough to create hairline cracks. "You're going to give the Madam a message. Tell her Alex is under my protection now." His hand closed around Granite's throat. "If she has a problem with that, she can take it up with me."

Smokey raised the gun again. Without looking, Kronos caught his wrist and twisted. A howl of pain followed the crack of breaking bone. The gun clattered to the frozen ground.

"That's for shooting at what's mine." Kronos's voice had dropped to a growl that barely sounded human. The air thrummed with power as he leaned closer to Granite. "Run back to your Madam and pray she's smarter than you."

He released them with deliberate slowness, rising to his full height. The enforcers scrambled backwards, the shadow one cradling his broken wrist while darkness swirled around them both. They disappeared into the growing night, leaving only scattered shards and disturbed earth to show they'd been there at all.

Kronos stood motionless for a moment, that supernatural energy still rolling off him in waves. When he turned toward my hiding spot, his eyes glowed in the darkness. Every instinct screamed at me to run away from him.

"Come here," he breathed.

My legs shook as I stood, using the tomb for support. The adrenaline was wearing off, letting me feel every place they'd struck. The taste of copper filled my mouth from my split lip.

He closed the distance between us in two long strides, tilting my face up to examine the damage. His touch was surprisingly gentle. "Are you alright, my darling?" he cooed, thumb brushing over my swelling cheek.

"I'm not yours," I managed, though the words lacked conviction.

His laugh was dark honey and danger. "Keep telling yourself that, little bunny." He scooped me up before I could protest, cradling me against his chest. "Now, let's get you cleaned up. Then you can explain why you were antagonizing the Madam's enforcers instead of waiting for midnight like a good boy."

"Put me down," I protested, but my body betrayed me, curling into his warmth against the bitter cold. "I can walk."

"Clearly," he said. "Since you did such a fine job of walking yourself into trouble." His heart beat steady and strong under my ear as he carried me through the cemetery. "Though I suppose I should be grateful. I was going to have to wait another few hours to see you."

The events of the last hour caught up with me all at once—the failed break-in, the enforcers, the gun—watching Kronos fight. My hands started shaking. "They were going to kill me," I whispered. "If you hadn't shown up—"

"But I did." His arms tightened around me. "And now they know better than to touch what's under my protection."

We reached his motorcycle, parked just outside the cemetery gates. He set me down, keeping one hand on my waist when my knees threatened to buckle.

"What happened to your bounty?" I asked, trying to distract myself from how close I'd come to dying.

His smile was sharp in the streetlight. "Handled. Permanently." He pulled his helmet off the bike. "Now hold on to me. I believe I promised you dinner before all this excitement."

His arms tightened around me, and I realized how close we were standing in the shadows of the cemetery. The adrenaline from the fight was still coursing through my system. I couldn't get my body to stop shaking.

"You're shivering," he murmured, one hand sliding up my back. "Are you scared or cold?"

"Both," I admitted, letting my forehead rest against his chest. His supernatural warmth seeped through my clothes, chasing away the winter chill. When his fingers tangled in my hair, tugging my head back to look at him, I couldn't help the small sound that escaped me.

"Such pretty prey," he growled, his thumb brushing over my split lip.

My breath hitched at the contact. The sting shot straight through me, pain melting into something darker that pooled hot and heavy in my gut. I couldn't help darting my tongue out to taste the salt of his skin, the copper of my blood. His eyes tracked the movement, pupils expanding until only a thin silver ring remained.

"Two months is a long time to wait," he said, voice dropping to that low register that vibrated straight through my chest and into places much lower.

When his mouth finally claimed mine, I whimpered. He was careful with my injured lip, but there was nothing gentle about the possession in his kiss. I tasted blood and need and the promise of what was to come. My head spun. Two months of filthy texts and heated voice messages hadn't prepared me for the reality of his touch. My hands fisted in his jacket, desperate to pull him closer, to erase any space between us.

I barely registered we were moving until cold marble slammed against my back—he'd walked me backward until I was pressed against the metal fence that surrounded the cemetery. The icy metal shocked through my clothes, making me arch away—and right into the furnaced heat of his body.

"We should take care of those bruises," he murmured against my jaw, the vibration of his voice making my skin prickle with goosebumps. "Getting you cleaned up and fed."

His hands slid under my coat, under my sweater, finding bare skin. I sucked in a sharp breath as his calloused fingers traced up my ribs. Every nerve ending sparked to life under his touch, my body remembering how good he could make me feel.

"Instead," he breathed against the sensitive spot below my ear, "all I can think about is marking you up myself."

I should've been appalled at the possessiveness in his voice. I should've pushed him away, reminded him we were in public, in a fucking cemetery of all places. Instead, I tilted my head to give him better access, my body betraying any shred of dignity I had left.

"Here?" The word came out a breathless gasp, nothing like the skeptical challenge I'd intended. My face burned at how transparent I was, how easily he could read my desperation after two months apart.

He caught my wrists in one large hand, pinning them above my head against the cold metal. My pulse thundered at the contact, at how effortlessly he restrained me, at how much I fucking liked it. The weight of him pressed me firmly against the tomb, his thigh sliding between mine, giving me just enough pressure to make my hips rock forward.

"Why not?" His breath was scalding against my throat, his free hand gripping my hip hard enough to bruise. "You *did* make me wait."

His teeth scraped over the sensitive skin where my neck met my shoulder, sending shocks straight to my core. I bit my lip to keep from moaning too loudly, suddenly very aware that we were outdoors, exposed.

"Breaking and entering. Making me track you down. Getting into trouble."

Each accusation came with another bite, another kiss, another mark that had me squirming against him, struggling to get closer despite the rational part of my brain screaming that this was insane. Two months without his touch had left me starved, desperate in ways I didn't want to admit even to myself.

"Such a naughty bunny," he purred, and god dammit, even that ridiculous nickname sent heat flooding through me. His thigh pressed higher between my legs, giving me the friction I craved, and I couldn't stop the embarrassing sound that escaped me as I rocked against him.

He smiled against my neck, the smug bastard. "I've missed those lovely sounds," he said, his hand sliding around to my lower back, pulling me tighter against him.

I gasped as his cock pressed against my hip, huge and rock-hard through his jeans. Holy fuck, I'd forgotten how big he was—or maybe I'd convinced myself I was exaggerating in my fantasies these past months. My mouth went dry at the feel of him, my body responding with a flood of heat that made me dizzy. Without thinking, I ground against him, seeking more friction, more pressure, more of everything he could give me.

"Kronos," I panted as his thigh pressed more deliberately between my legs, the friction incredible but not enough, never enough. My face burned as I realized how close I was already, how easily he could make me cum right here in public. The winter air stung my overheated skin. "Someone could—"

"See?" His laugh was dark against my skin. "Let them. Let them all see who you belong to."

"Marshmallow," I breathed against his neck, my heart still racing.

Kronos pulled back, his hands moving to cradle my face with infinite gentleness. The predatory heat in his eyes shifted to concern as he studied my expression. "Are you alright? Did I hurt you?"

"No, no, you didn't," I assured him, feeling heat creep up my neck. "I just..." I gestured at our surroundings—the cemetery, the open night air. "Not here. Please."

His thumb brushed softly over my unbruised cheek. "Of course. I'm sorry. I got carried away." He pressed a gentle kiss to my forehead. "Do you still want to come back to my place? We can wait if you need time."

"I want to," I said, my voice small but certain. "I've missed you. I just..." I laughed awkwardly, glancing at the ornate tomb behind us. "Prefer walls, privacy, and maybe not being surrounded by gravestones?"

His answering chuckle was warm and understanding, all traces of that earlier predatory edge gone. "Fair enough." He stepped back, keeping one steadying hand on my waist. "Let's get you warmed up and looked after properly, then."

Chapter Eleven

Bound by Silk

The ride back to Kronos's brownstone was a blur of city lights and his solid warmth against my back. The adrenaline from our cemetery encounter was wearing off, leaving my bruised ribs aching, but my mind surprisingly clear.

I leaned against the kitchen island, mesmerized by the practiced efficiency of Kronos's movements. His kitchen was nothing like I'd expected—no sterile professional chef's setup, but a lived-in space with copper pots hanging from a rack above a massive gas range, well-worn wooden cutting boards stained with the ghosts of past meals, and bundles of dried herbs dangling from ceiling hooks. The walls were a warm terracotta that caught the golden light spilling from vintage pendant lamps, making the whole space glow like the inside of a hearth.

A collection of ancient cooking utensils hung on one wall—some I couldn't even guess the purpose of—alongside what looked like an antique cleaver that had seen several lifetimes of use. Spices lined open shelving in mismatched jars labeled in a script I didn't recognize, filling the air with scents that transported me somewhere I'd never been but somehow felt familiar.

He was chopping vegetables for gyros with mesmerizing precision, the knife an extension of his hand. Each slice was perfect, uniform, creating a small mountain of diced tomatoes, onions, and something green and…sticky. Not once did he look down at his hands. Instead, he was fixed on me, watching my reaction to the space, to him, like I was the most fascinating thing in the room.

He caught me staring and the corner of his mouth quirked up, sending an unwanted flutter through my stomach. My own attempts at cooking ended in disaster—the last time I'd tried to make anything more complicated than toast, I'd nearly taken off a finger. The memory of blood spreading across my cutting board, the panicky trip to the emergency room where I'd had to glamour the receptionist to move me up the list because I couldn't afford insurance... After that, I'd stuck to what I knew: using my glamour to convince people to feed me. Gas station attendants with their sad rotating hot dogs, wait staff who could be charmed into 'forgetting' to ring up dessert, anyone who might take pity on a pretty face when I was broke and desperate.

The sound of Kronos's knife hitting the wooden board created a hypnotic rhythm that filled the kitchen—*chop, chop, scrape* as he gathered the pieces, then repeat. A pot of something simmered on the stove, bubbling occasionally and releasing a steam that smelled of garlic and lemon. My stomach growled, loud enough in the quiet kitchen that there was no way he hadn't heard it with his preternatural senses.

"What's going on in that head of yours?" Kronos asked, setting down his knife. "You've gone somewhere far away."

"Just thinking about cooking," I said, trying to keep my voice light. "My mom used to make these amazing pistachio pancakes when I was little."

The memory hit me harder than I expected—a bright Sunday morning, the scent of vanilla and nuts filling our tiny kitchen, her humming some old Puerto Rican song as she flipped each perfect circle. The familiar ache settled in my chest, the one that always appeared when I allowed myself to remember.

"She was Puerto Rican?" Kronos asked, his tone casual, but his eyes watchful. "When was the last time you saw her? Perhaps we could visit sometime."

I stared down at the vegetables, running my finger along the grain of the wooden cutting board. The question was innocent enough, but it poked at wounds I usually kept bandaged and hidden.

"She died," The words scraped my throat. "Three years after my father kicked me out. I wasn't there."

Kronos set his knife down then, coming to stand behind me at the counter. His chest pressed against my back, a solid warmth that somehow made it easier to speak. "I'm sorry," he said, no platitudes or awkward questions.

"She was…" I swallowed hard, surprised to want to tell him more. "She was this funny, vibrant woman who could light up a room just by walking into it. Literally, sometimes. The will-o'-wisp heritage comes from her side." I gestured toward my eyes. "Hence the blue. She had the same eyes."

His hand settled on my hip. "What was her cooking like?"

A small smile tugged at my lips despite everything. "*Buenísimo.* She could turn the simplest ingredients into something magical. My favorite was her *arroz con gandules*—rice with pigeon peas. She'd always have me be her, *manito*—little helper—in the kitchen, letting me stir the pot or add the spices." The memory was so vivid I could almost taste the savory rice, feel the steam warming my face as I stood on a chair to reach the stove. "She'd tell me stories while we cooked, legends about our ancestors and magic."

I didn't realize I was crying until Kronos turned me to face him, brushing away a tear I hadn't felt fall. "She taught me that food was love," I admitted, the words barely audible. "That feeding someone was a way of caring for their soul, not just their body."

The letter about her death had arrived three years later, a single page of my sister's stiff handwriting that held none of her grief but all of her resentment. Tucked inside was *Mami's* rosary—amber beads worn smooth from decades of prayers, the silver crucifix tarnished but still beautiful. I knew Penelope must have hated parting with it; she'd always coveted it, always thought it should be hers someday. But *Mami* had left it to me in her will. Now it stayed wrapped around a glass candle in my apartment, part of the small altar I'd built in the corner of my bedroom. On All Souls Day, Three Kings Day and her birthday, I'd leave out her favorite wine and foods—*arroz con gandules, flan, or turron* she'd spend all day making for special occasions. Sometimes I'd catch myself talking to her photo, telling her about my day as if she were still there to listen.

"A woman after my own heart," he said. "I wish I could have met her."

"Me too." Another memory surfaced—my mother's face the day my father threw me out, her eyes red-rimmed and pleading as she slipped me all the cash from her secret stash. She hadn't been able to stand against him, but she'd loved me. It had been the last time I'd seen her alive.

"She would have liked you," I said, surprising myself with the certainty in my voice.

Kronos's laugh was soft, his hands settling on my shoulders. "Did she also teach you how to charm your way into extra fries, or was that a talent you developed on your own?"

The question eased the tightness in my chest, offering a graceful way back from the edge of too many painful memories. "That was pure survival instinct," I said, grateful for the shift. "When you're twenty, broke, and living out of your car, you get creative."

His expression shifted at that—something flashing behind those silver eyes too quickly for me to interpret. "Well," he said, guiding my hands back to the cutting board, "tonight I get to charm you." His hands settled over mine, showing me how to curl my fingers to protect them from the blade. "See how the knife rocks? Let it do the work." His voice had taken on an exaggerated instructional tone that made me smile despite myself. "This, my dear student, is the ancient and sacred art of not mutilating vegetables."

"Is that what they taught you in Greece?" I asked, leaning back against him as we worked, grateful for how easily he'd guided us past my unexpected vulnerability.

"Mm. Right after 'how to brood mysteriously' and before 'tactical deployment of sexy accent for maximum effect.'" His lips brushed my ear. "Though I must say, watching you try to seduce a gas station attendant for frozen burritos sounds entertaining."

I stiffened. That had been right after we met. "What?"

"You talk in your sleep." He reached past me for another tomato. "Now, observe the proper angle of attack. The tomato is our prey. We must approach with stealth and precision."

A laugh bubbled up from my chest, surprising me. "You're ridiculous."

"Am I?" His free hand slid to my hip, steadying me as we continued chopping. "I'll have you know tomato hunting is a very serious business. Now, for the grape leaves—those require a more delicate touch."

I pinched the leaves, attempting to tuck the leaves into a burrito shape, but it fell apart as soon as I released it.

"You're doing it wrong," he murmured against my ear, though his hands stayed gentle over mine as we tried to roll the stuffed grape leaves. "Too loose. They'll fall apart in the pot."

"Maybe if someone wasn't distracting me," I shot back, very aware of how he'd pressed closer, his chest solid against my back. The kitchen smelled amazing—herbs and spices mixed with the scent of cedar and storm that always clung to his skin. It was strange how comfortable this felt, how easily we'd fallen into this domestic scene after watching him break a man's wrist less than an hour ago.

"Distracting? Me?" His laugh rumbled through both of us. "I'm being helpful. Look—" He guided my fingers to fold the leaf tighter. "Like swaddling a tiny, delicious baby."

"That's a disturbing way to think about food." I leaned into him, letting his warmth chase away the lingering chill of the cemetery. There was something soothing about this—his hands directing mine, teaching instead of demanding. It reminded me of watching my mother in the kitchen, though I pushed that thought away before it could sting.

"Says the man who used to glamour his way into extra fries." His teeth grazed my ear, sending a shock straight to my dick. "Besides, I seem to recall someone being very interested in my texts about rope."

Heat flooded my cheeks as fragments of those messages hit me—him promising to tie my wrists so tight I couldn't move for shit, spreading my legs wide open with rough rope, positioning knots right where they'd dig into all the spots that made me squirm. Last night's text was the worst—or best, depending on how you looked at it. Him describing how he'd tie me up like a fucking present, ass in the air, face shoved into the mattress, arms wrenched behind my back while he teased me for hours, never letting me cum until I was practically crying for it.

I hardened against my zipper. Fuck. I shifted awkwardly, hoping he wouldn't notice how easily he got to me. For months, those filthy messages had been my nightly ritual—phone in one hand, dick in the other, coming so hard I had to bite my pillow to keep from waking Twyla next door. Nobody had ever made me this fucking desperate before, and the bastard knew it.

"The food's going to burn."

"Not for hours yet." His hands stilled over mine, the half-rolled grape leaf forgotten. "These need to simmer. And I can think of several ways to pass the time…"

The grape leaves were rolled—some more neatly than others—and simmering with the rest of dinner when Kronos caught my hand. "Come with me," he said, his voice carrying that gentle authority that made my pulse quicken. "There's something I want to show you."

I followed him into the living room, where the hunting scenes in the paintings were calmer tonight, less predatory. I wondered if they only looked alive when I was drinking. Three coils of rope lay arranged on the coffee table, each one catching the light differently—deep royal purple that shone like silk, stark white that looked sturdy but flexible, and a rich red that was unyielding.

"I've been thinking about this since that night in the alley," he said, his thumb tracing circles on my wrist. "How to introduce you to this properly." He led me closer to the table. "Feel them. See which one calls to you."

The intensity in his voice made my mouth go dry, but there was no pressure in his touch, no demand.

My fingers trailed over each rope in turn. The red was too intimidating, almost severe in its stiffness. The white felt like a compromise, neither too harsh nor too soft. The purple...I lifted it, letting it slide through my fingers.

"This one," I said, surprised by how steady my voice was. The texture reminded me of his silk sheets from that first night, luxurious and somehow safe in the aftermath.

His smile was approving. "Excellent choice. The softest one—perfect for beginners." He took the rope, but didn't move to use it yet. "Tonight isn't about sex. It's about trust. About feeling safe enough to let go."

I swallowed hard, watching his hands work with the rope. "And if I want to stop?"

"Then we stop." He showed me a simple knot, demonstrating how it would work. "One pull here releases everything. The end stays in your hand the whole time." His fingers brushed mine as he explained. "You're in control of this, Alex. I'm just here to guide you."

"How does it work?" I asked, torn between nervousness and curiosity. "The rope, I mean. The...technique?"

"First, I check circulation points." He traced the veins on my wrist with gentle fingers. "Make sure nothing's too tight. We go slow. I ask how you're feeling. You tell me the moment anything feels wrong. May I?" he asked, holding up the purple rope. When I nodded, he moved behind me, his chest pressed to my back like when we were cooking. "Hands in front, palms together, like you're praying."

I followed his instruction, trying to control my breathing as he brought the rope around my wrists.

"How's that feel?" His fingers checked the spaces between rope and skin. "Not too tight?"

"No, it's...nice." The word felt inadequate. "Different than I expected."

"Rope is an art form," he murmured, his breath warm against my ear. "It's about connection, trust. The Japanese call it Shibari—the beauty of binding." His hands moved to my shoulders, massaging gently. "Feel how the rope moves when you do? But the end is always in your control."

He was right—I could feel the release knot against my palm, easily within reach. Something about that simple fact made the rest of the tension drain from my shoulders.

"Good boy," he praised. "Now, I believe dinner's almost ready. Let me take care of you."

He guided me to sit on one of the plush leather chairs at his dining table, the rope a constant gentle presence around my wrists. The scents from the kitchen were mouthwatering—herbs and spices I couldn't name mixing with garlic and roasted meat.

"How are your hands feeling?" he asked, checking the rope again. "Any numbness? Tingling?"

"No, they're fine." I flexed my fingers to show the rope moving smoothly with the motion. "It's almost...c omforting?"

He set a plate in front of me. The gyros looked like something from a food magazine, nothing like the street cart versions I used to charm my way into getting. "That's the point. Safe." He picked up a piece of the meat, holding it to my lips. "Open."

Heat crept up my neck at being fed like this, but I parted my lips. The flavors exploded across my tongue—perfectly seasoned lamb, the tang of yogurt sauce, fresh herbs.

"Good?" He brushed his thumb across my lower lip, catching a drop of sauce.

I nodded, surprised by how intimate this felt—more intimate than some of the sexual things we'd done. "Where did you learn to cook like this?"

"My grandmother taught me," he said, preparing another bite. "In a little village outside Athens. She believed food was another form of caring for people." His eyes held a faraway look.

The rope shifted against my wrists as I adjusted my position. The combination of good food and Kronos's undivided attention was doing something to my head—making me relaxed and reckless at the same time. It reminded me of being drunk but clearer, like my usual filters were dissolving. His silver eyes caught mine, and something about the way he looked at me—like I was something precious—made my chest tight.

The question that had been nagging at me for weeks suddenly felt urgent. Maybe it was the rope making me feel secure, or maybe it was hearing him talk about his past for once. Whatever it was, I couldn't hold it back anymore.

"Why do you keep calling me bunny?" I asked, the words tumbling out before I could stop them.

Kronos paused with the fork halfway to my mouth, that familiar amused expression spreading across his face.

"Does it bother you?" There was genuine curiosity in his voice, despite the smirk playing on his lips.

"No, I'm just curious," I said, feeling heat creep up my neck. *God, what a stupid time to ask this question, while literally tied up at his dining table.* "Just wondering why a bunny, of all things?"

He set down the fork and slid a finger under the rope at my wrist, tugging slightly. The casual way he handled the bindings made my stomach flip. He was so confident, like he'd done this a thousand times before. Maybe he had.

"Do you know what someone who enjoys being tied up is called in certain circles?" His eyes locked with mine, watching for my reaction.

I shook my head, feeling even more out of my depth than usual.

His smile widened, revealing those sharp teeth. "A rope bunny," he said, picking up the fork again and offering me another bite.

Before I could process his answer, he leaned closer, his voice dropping to that register that made my insides turn to liquid. "Seeing you trussed up like this, unable to run away, waiting for me to devour you however I please..." His eyes darkened as they traveled over the ropes binding my wrists. "Nothing makes my mouth water more."

The food went down the wrong way as his words registered. I choked, coughing and sputtering while he chuckled and patted my back, his expression one of pure self-satisfaction.

"Didn't realize it would be such a shock," he said, though the gleam in his eyes made it clear he was enjoying my reaction. "Water?"

I nodded, still trying to catch my breath, my face burning. The ropes felt different against my skin, the nickname taking on meanings I hadn't considered. Rope bunny. And the way he'd said 'devour' had sent a jolt of heat straight to my groin.

The familiar weight of shame tried to creep in—I shouldn't need this, shouldn't want to be taken care of like this—but his next words scattered those thoughts.

"You've spent so long trying to take care of your-self," he murmured, fingers tracing the rope's pattern. "Let someone take care of you for once."

"I'm not very good at that," I admitted, accepting another bite of food.

"I've noticed." His smile held no judgment. "That's why we practice. Like with the cooking—small steps, building trust." He checked the circulation in my fingers again. "How are you feeling?"

"Safe," I whispered, surprising myself with the truth of it.

His thumb brushed across my lower lip again, lin-gering this time. "Good boy." The praise made heat pool in my stomach. "Though I must say, watching you all tied up and pliant is testing my resolve about not touching you tonight."

I shifted in my seat, very aware of how his eyes darkened at the movement. "Maybe that was my plan all along."

"Tease," he purred softly, fingers trailing down my neck. "Here you are, all wrapped up like a present." His other hand checked the ropes again, professional even as his touch made me shiver. "We're building something here, darling. Something that requires patience."

"Says the man who's been sending me detailed de-scriptions of how he plans to tie me up."

"Consider those previews of coming attractions." He offered another bite of food, but pulled back just as I leaned forward. "If you're good." His hand slid to the back of my neck, thumb tracing circles just under my hairline.

"And you can be very good, can't you?" His voice had dropped lower, making my breath catch. "When you want to be."

"Sometimes." I tested the ropes, not trying to escape, just feeling how they moved. The end was still in my hand, but I had no desire to pull it. "Though you seem to like it when I'm not."

"Mmhmm." He leaned closer, his breath hot against my ear. "I like the chase." His free hand traced the rope pattern around my wrists. "But seeing you give in willingly? That's something else entirely."

The next bite he offered was from the stuffed grape leaves. His fingers lingered against my lips longer than necessary, and I couldn't resist catching one with my teeth. The sound he made was almost a growl.

"Careful, bunny," he warned, though his eyes sparked with heat. "Keep that up and I might forget about taking things slow." He murmured, deliberately keeping his hands away from the release knot. "The choice is yours. Just like it's always been."

I looked down at the tab resting in my palm—the one he hadn't touched once since placing it there. Something about that deliberate respect for my control made my chest tight. With a gentle tug, the rope slid away like water.

He took my hands then, massaging each wrist with careful attention, checking circulation one last time. "Perfect," he praised. "You did so well tonight. Come lay with me?" he asked, rising and holding out his hand. When I took it, he led me to the massive leather sofa, settling into the corner and drawing me against his chest. His supernatural warmth and the heavy meal made my eyelids feel impossibly heavy.

"Stay," he murmured into my hair, pulling a throw blanket over us both. It was soft as clouds against my skin.

I wanted to protest—I had work tomorrow, clothes to change, a dozen reasons to go home. But his heartbeat was steady under my ear, his fingers carding through my hair in a hypnotic rhythm. For once, I let myself just be held, just be cared for.

The last thing I registered before drifting off was his lips pressing softly against my temple, and the quiet whisper.

"Sweet dreams, my love."

Chapter Twelve

MARKED

I wiped my sweaty palms on my jeans for the third time in as many minutes, surveying my handiwork with critical eyes. The apartment looked nothing like its usual self. I'd pushed my worn furniture against the walls, making space for the makeshift pottery studio I'd assembled in the center of the room. Two pottery wheels sat on thick plastic sheeting, surrounded by milk crates I'd turned upside down to serve as tables. Clay tools, buckets of water, and various glazes were arranged with the same careful precision I used for my leatherworking tools.

String lights crisscrossed the ceiling, casting a warm glow that was both romantic and practical enough to work by. I'd 'borrowed' them from Twyla's holiday decoration stash, along with the small electric kiln that now hummed in the corner. It had taken some creative rewiring to make sure I wouldn't blow a fuse, but the result looked...pretty damn good, actually. I surveyed the room, noticing the darker corners the string lights didn't reach. With a subtle flick of my wrist, I sent three small orbs of blue light to hover near the ceiling, providing additional soft illumination. They looked natural enough to be mistaken for clever modern lighting fixtures, but would provide just the right ambiance. One settled near the Puerto Rican flag I'd thumb tacked above my workbench, illuminating its red, white, and blue pattern that was one of the few constants in each place I'd lived.

My phone buzzed with a text notification.

Kronos: *Parking now. Need me to bring anything up?*

This was the first time I'd planned anything for us. It felt significant, somehow. Like I was opening a door I kept firmly shut. It felt nice to have some control over the space for once.

Alex: *Just yourself.*

I glanced at the bottle of wine breathing on the counter—a decent red I'd splurged on after Twyla insisted that "Two Buck Chuck isn't appropriate date wine, Alex, for God's sake." Next to it sat the cheese and charcuterie board I'd assembled with perhaps excessive care. YouTube tutorials had taught me how to fan apple slices and roll prosciutto into little roses. It looked almost professional, if you ignored the uneven cuts on the cheese.

A knock at the door sent my heart rate spiking. I took a deep breath, reminded myself that I'd seen this man naked for god's sake, and opened the door.

Kronos stood there in dark jeans and a forest green Henley that made his red hair look like burnished copper. He'd brought flowers—not roses, but a wild-looking arrangement of stems I didn't recognize, tied with simple twine.

"For you," he said, handing them to me with a small smile. "You've been busy."

I stepped aside to let him in, hoping the glow from the string lights disguised my blush. "It's nothing fancy."

"It's perfect," he replied, taking in the transformed apartment. His eyes lingered on the pottery wheels, then shifted to me with amusement. "So this is why you've been so secretive."

"I overheard Twyla talking about those wine and painting classes...and I thought, hey, why not?" I shrugged, aiming for casual despite the nervous flutter in my stomach. "Figured it was time I taught you something for a change."

His smile widened at that. "I look forward to being your student." There was something in his eyes—a warmth that made my chest tight. "Though I should warn you, I have no idea what we're doing."

I relaxed a fraction, setting the flowers in a mason jar of water. At least he's not like a master already. That would have been a little embarrassing. "Don't worry. I'll be gentle with you."

His laugh was low, rich. "A novel experience."

I poured the wine, handed him a glass, and gestured to the charcuterie board. "Food first? Or do you want to jump right in?"

"Let's eat," he said, accepting both the wine and a small plate. "I'm curious to hear how you learned this. It wasn't mentioned in any of our...previous conversations."

"Community center class when I was fourteen," I explained, focusing on arranging food on my plate rather than meeting his eyes. "My mom thought I needed constructive ways to channel my energy. It was that or soccer, and I wasn't exactly team sports material."

"I can't imagine you taking direction well," he agreed, popping an olive into his mouth.

I snorted. "You'd be surprised what I can take when properly motivated."

His eyes darkened at that, but he just sipped his wine, letting the comment slide by with admirable restraint. "And pottery stuck with you?"

"It's therapeutic," I said, surprised at how easy it was to talk about this with him. "Working with your hands, creating something from nothing. Kind of like leatherworking, but...messier."

We finished our food in companionable conversation, and I felt the last of my tension drain away. This was good. Different from our usual dynamic, but good.

"Shall we begin?" he asked, catching me staring.

I cleared my throat, setting our plates aside. "Yeah, let's get to it."

I guided him to one of the pottery wheels, positioning myself at the other. "First, we need to prepare the clay." I handed him a lump of gray stoneware clay, taking another for myself. "You want to knead it like bread dough, work out any air bubbles."

He followed my lead, those powerful hands working the clay with careful attention. I tried not to stare at the way his forearms flexed with each movement, the way his fingers pressed and shaped the material. It was almost hypnotic. Also, veiny arms, hello.

"Like this?" he asked, and I realized I'd been silent too long.

"Yeah, you're doing great," I said, grateful he was too focused to see me breathing a little heavier. I needed to get a grip. "Now we need to center it on the wheel."

This was the tricky part, and I wasn't surprised when Kronos's clay wobbled as the wheel spun. What did surprise me was the flash of frustration that crossed his face—quickly controlled, but definitely there. The mighty Primal, undone by a lump of wet clay.

"Here," I said, moving behind him. "It's all about finding the center." I placed my hands over his, guiding them to the spinning clay. "Feel that? When it's centered, there's almost no resistance."

His body was warm against my chest with his sandwiched between my arms. I could feel the slight tension in his broad shoulders as he concentrated.

"Relax your grip a little," I cooed, bending his elbow a little. "Let the clay move with you, not against you. There you go."

The clay smoothed under our combined touch, finding its center on the wheel. When I stepped back, Kronos looked up at me and raised a brow.

"You're an excellent teacher," he said, and the simple praise made something warm unfurl in my chest.

"Now the fun part," I said, moving back to my wheel. "We're going to open the clay and start shaping it. Watch me first."

I demonstrated on my wheel, enjoying the familiar motions—pressing my thumbs into the center of the spinning clay, gradually widening the opening, pulling the walls up with careful pressure. Muscle memory took over, and I found myself lost in the process, barely aware of Kronos watching until I looked up to find his eyes fixed on me with intense focus.

"Your turn," I said, my voice coming out a little rougher than intended.

He positioned his hands as I had shown him, but the clay warped. His brow furrowed as he tried to correct it, only making the wobble worse.

"Easy," I cautioned. "You're using too much pressure."

"I thought pressure was the point," he snapped, as the clay continued to resist him.

I bit back a smile. "Gentle pressure. Consistent. Like...when you're checking rope ties. Firm but not forceful."

He adjusted his approach, but the clay had already lost its center. It spun off-kilter, and when he tried to correct it, the entire lump collapsed, sending a spray of watery clay across his chest and face.

The sight of the always-perfect Kronos with gray mud splattered across his face, looking bewildered, broke something loose inside me. "I'm sorry," I gasped between chuckles. "*Dios mío, mírate!*" I laughed, unable to contain myself. "You look like you lost a fight with a mud puddle."

He looked down at himself, then back at me, and a slow smile spread across his mud-speckled features. Holy shit. With clay streaking his chiseled cheekbones and that genuine smile lighting up his eyes, he was the most beautiful thing I'd ever seen. Not perfect-beautiful like in a magazine, but real-beautiful. Raw. My chest hurt looking at him like this.

"I believe I need more instruction," he said, his voice carrying that a tint of humor.

Before I could retreat, he reached out and smeared a handful of wet clay across my cheek. "There," he said, satisfaction in his tone. "Much better."

"Oh, it's like that, is it?" I grabbed a handful of clay, but he caught my wrist before I could retaliate.

"Careful, little bunny," he warned, though his eyes sparkled with mischief. "You're dealing with a predator."

"A very dirty predator," I countered, using my free hand to smear another streak of clay across his jaw.

His laugh was startled, genuine in a way that made me bite my lip to keep from laughing. Then he lunged, grabbing both my wrists and spinning me until my back pressed against the nearby wall, careful to avoid my shelves of supplies but still pinning me.

"Now I have you," he murmured, his face close to mine. Clay dripped from his temple, sliding along his cheek. Without overthinking it, I leaned forward and kissed him. It was playful, almost sweet, my lips catching his and drawing him in.

He stilled for a moment, then released my wrists to cradle my face instead, deepening the kiss with careful attention. The taste of wine and clay and him mingled on my tongue, making me dizzy.

When we broke apart, his silver eyes had that molten quality that made my stomach flip. "I think I like your teaching methods," he whispered. "It brings out the brat in you."

I smiled, trying not to squirm under his attention and failing. "You're a disaster at pottery."

"I prefer to think of it as creative expression," he quipped, glancing at the collapsed lump of clay on his wheel.

"Is that what you're calling it?" I laughed, the sound coming easily.

We were both a mess—clay-streaked and disheveled—but I couldn't remember the last time I'd felt this light. This...happy. The realization was both thrilling and terrifying. Happiness was easily stolen away.

"Let me help clean up," he said, releasing me and looking at the splatters of clay that had reached the wall and floor during his mishap.

"It's okay," I protested, but he was already gathering towels from the stack I'd prepared.

"I insist," he said as he set himself to scooping splattered clay from where chunks had painted the walls.

We worked together in comfortable silence, wiping down surfaces and gathering tools. When our hands met, reaching for the same towel, he didn't pull away, just let his fingers linger against mine for a moment longer than necessary.

"I should shower," I said when we'd finished, gesturing at the clay still speckling both of us. "You can use it after…"

The invitation hovered unspoken between us. In the weeks since that first night on his couch, we'd developed a pattern—sex at his place, but always with me returning to my apartment afterward. I'd never asked him to stay here, and I'd always left his place before dawn. My place had been off-limits…until today.

"Or," I continued before I could lose my nerve, focusing on arranging clean towels, "you could just stay. If you want." I risked a glance at him, heart hammering. "It's late, and…"

His smile was soft, something almost tender in his eyes. "Of course, my love."

I pretended not to notice how his hands tightened around the broom, turning away to hide whatever might be visible on my face. "Great. I'll just…" I gestured awkwardly toward the bathroom.

His hand caught mine, tugging me back. "Alex," he said softly, waiting until I met his eyes. "Thank you.

For tonight." Like he understood what it had cost me to open this door, to let him into this part of my life. Letting people in had always been difficult and often dangerous for me.

"It was just pottery," I said, deflecting with a shrug. "Not very successful, in your case."

"It was perfect," he corrected, pressing a kiss to my clay-smudged forehead. "Now go shower. I'll finish tidying up here."

I turned the water as hot as I could stand it, letting steam fill the small bathroom as I peeled off my clay-stiffened clothes. The running water had barely begun to rinse the first layer of clay from my skin when the bathroom door opened.

Through the fogged glass, I watched Kronos's silhouette as he pulled his shirt over his head, revealing the carved lines of his torso. I took a step back to get a better view of him, only being able to see the outline of him from the chest down.

"Mind if I join you?" His voice was casual as he stepped out of his jeans.

"Please do." I moved back, making room as he slid the shower door open and stepped in. My tiny shower stall wasn't built for someone his size, let alone two people, but that just meant there was no avoiding the press of his skin against mine. I took in the firm curve of his ass as he scooted past me to reach the back of the shower.

"You've got clay..." His fingers traced my jawline, brushing at a stubborn spot near my ear. The simple touch sent delicious chills racing down my spine. "Everywhere, actually."

"So do you," I managed, watching water sluice over his shoulders, turning the dried clay to rivulets of gray that traced the contours of his chest.

He reached past me for the soap, his chest brushing mine in a way that could not possibly be accidental. "Turn around," he instructed, his voice dropping low and sultry. "Let me help."

I obeyed without thinking, the warm spray hitting my chest as his hands, slick with soap, worked across my shoulders. His touch was different tonight—less commanding, more attentive–like he was mapping every inch of me.

"You're good with your hands," I murmured as his fingers worked the tension from my neck, sliding down to trace my spine.

His soft laugh rumbled against my back as he pressed closer. "I have many talents."

"So I've noticed." I leaned back into him, letting my head fall against his shoulder. The soap made his skin slick against mine, creating a delicious friction with every slight movement. Steam curled around us, wrapping us in our own private world where nothing existed beyond the shower's glass walls. His hands glided over my chest, leaving trails of warmth that lingered long after his touch moved on.

The hot water drummed against my collarbone, rivulets finding paths down my torso only to be redirected by his exploring fingers. Each sweep of his hands washed away a little more of my usual restraint. The clay was gone now, but he kept touching, kept exploring.

When his hand drifted lower across my stomach, my muscles jumped under his touch. The gentle scrape of his calloused palm against sensitive skin sent lightning racing up my spine. A sound escaped me—needy, desperate—echoing off the bathroom tiles before I could swallow it back.

His breath was hot against my ear, a stark contrast to the cooling water. "I've been thinking about touching you like this for weeks," he murmured, his voice a physical thing that vibrated through me where we pressed together. "Ever since you invited me over."

My thoughts scattered like water droplets, impossible to gather as his fingers traced teasing patterns along my hip bones. Every nerve ending sparked to life, my body arching into his touch without conscious permission. I couldn't remember why I'd ever hesitated to let him into this part of my life, couldn't recall a single reason this wasn't the best idea I'd ever had.

"Is this okay?" he asked, lips brushing my ear. That was new—him asking instead of taking.

"God, yes," I breathed, turning in his arms to capture his mouth with mine.

The kiss was desperate, savage, my tongue sliding against his as I tasted soap and something darker, something primal that belonged only to him. My hands found purchase on his slick chest, tracing every ridge and valley of muscle before sliding up to tangle in his wet hair. I tugged hard, and the growl that vibrated through his chest wasn't human—it was pure predator, and it sent a violent shudder straight to my core.

He slammed me against the shower wall, the cold tile a brutal shock against my overheated skin. The contrast tore a gasp from my throat, my back arching away from the chill and into the scorching heat of him. His body pinned mine, hard everywhere—chest, thighs, cock—as water cascaded over both of us, turning the soap into a slick barrier that made every slide of his body against mine feel like torture.

"Kronos," I barely recognized my voice as his mouth left mine to trace a burning path down my neck. My fingers dug into his shoulders hard enough to leave marks, desperate for an anchor as he bit down on that spot below my ear that always made me collapse.

His hands were everywhere at once, possessive and demanding, claiming every inch of me with bruising intensity. When his fingers wrapped around my cock, slick with soap and water, I nearly lost it right there. My head slammed back against the tile, vision going white at the edges.

"Let me hear you," he demanded, his voice rough with barely contained savagery. "I want to hear what I do to you."

I couldn't have held back if my life depended on it. Every merciless stroke of his hand ripped sounds from my throat I'd never heard myself make—broken, animal noises that bounced off the tile walls and came back to mock me. His silver eyes burned into mine, watching every twitch, every gasp, adjusting his pace and pressure until I was a trembling, incoherent mess.

Just when I thought I couldn't take any more, when I was right on the razor's edge, he dropped to his knees with predatory grace, water streaming over his shoulders as he looked up at me with eyes that glowed like molten metal. "Hold on," was all the warning I got before his mouth replaced his hand.

The wet, searing heat of him engulfed me. My vision blacked out for a second, and I grabbed blindly for support, knocking bottles and soap everywhere as my legs threatened to give out. The sight of him on his knees, water sluicing down that perfect body while he took me apart like it was his divine fucking purpose in life, was too much to process.

"Fuck—Kronos—I can't." Words failed me as his tongue did something that should be illegal in all fifty states. His strong hands gripped my hips with bruising force, holding me in place as he worked me with ruthless precision.

It was the combination that destroyed me—his mouth, his hands digging into my hips, and those inhuman silver eyes locked on mine, refusing to let me hide as he watched me fall apart. The orgasm hit like a freight train. My entire body convulsed, pleasure so intense it bordered on pain consuming me until there was nothing left but sensation.

By the time I clawed my way back to consciousness, the water had gone ice cold, but I couldn't feel anything beyond the aftershocks still rippling through me. My legs had given out, and Kronos was holding me up against the tile, his expression almost reverent as he watched me struggle to remember how breathing worked.

"Perfect," he murmured, pushing wet hair from my face with surprising gentleness. The contrast between the savage hunger of moments before and this tender touch made my throat tight with emotions I wasn't ready to name.

I felt hollowed out, rebuilt, and marked in ways that went far deeper than physical. Whatever this was between us had just crossed into territory I'd never navigated before, and some distant part of me recognized I should be terrified. Instead, I just let my head fall against his shoulder, surrendering to the strange peace that came after being so thoroughly claimed.

Later, he sat on my bed wrapped in a towel. He lounged in my sweatpants that barely reached his ankles, his chest still damp from our shower.

"What are you thinking?" he asked, catching me staring.

"That I didn't expect tonight to end like this," I admitted. "But I'm not complaining."

His smile was slow. "Good, because I'm not finished with you yet." He sat beside me, the mattress dipping under his weight. "In fact, I was thinking we might go shopping soon."

"Shopping?" The change of subject threw me. "For what?"

His fingers traced the edge of my towel. "Something special. For us." His eyes held mine, heat and promise in their silver depths. "There's a store I know that carries items I think you'd enjoy. Things I'd very much like to use on you."

The implication sent heat flooding through me all over again. "Oh."

"But only if you're interested," he added, and there was that newness again—the careful attention to my comfort, my consent.

I thought about the texts we'd exchanged over the past few weeks, about the things he'd described in explicit detail, about how completely undone I'd been in the shower just moments ago.

"Show me," I said, leaning in to brush my lips against his. "I want to see."

His smile was dark with satisfaction. "Soon," he promised, tugging me into his lap. "Very soon."

I woke to the scent of coffee and something sweet baking. The sheets beside me were empty but still warm. I stretched, savoring the lingering ache in my muscles from the night before.

"Look who's finally awake," Kronos said from the doorway, a steaming mug in one hand and something tucked under his arm. The morning light caught his hair, turning it to burnished copper as he approached.

I made an unintelligible noise and reached out with grabby hands. "Nngh. Coffee."

His low chuckle vibrated through the room as he handed over the mug. I wrapped my fingers around it like it contained the elixir of life, breathing in the steam before taking a desperate sip. The caffeine hit my system, bringing my brain back online.

He sat on the edge of the bed, watching me with amusement as I gulped down half the mug before coming up for air.

"I got you something," he said, a note in his voice I'd never heard before—softer, less certain.

From behind his back, he produced a plush bunny with cream-colored fur so soft it looked unreal. Floppy ears framed a stitched face with a gentle expression, and around its neck was a tiny purple silk ribbon—the exact shade of the rope he'd first used on me.

"Seriously?" I groaned, but couldn't fight the smile tugging at my lips. "You're never letting this bunny thing go, are you?"

"Never," he confirmed, placing it in my lap with surprising gentleness. His eyes tracked my reaction, silver irises catching the morning light.

I ran my fingers over the impossibly soft fur, something unfamiliar tightening in my chest. The sensation was almost uncomfortable—not pain exactly, but an ache that made it hard to swallow. No one had given me something so pointlessly sweet since I was a kid. It was stupid and sentimental and exactly the sort of thing I would have mocked before him.

"Thank you," I said under my breath, fingers still tracing the bunny's ears. I couldn't look at him. "It's...I like it."

His smile transformed his entire face, softening the predatory lines into something that made my stomach flip. He leaned forward and pressed his lips to my forehead, lingering there. I closed my eyes, breathing in the scent of him.

"Do I need to worry about competition?" he asked, pulling back to eye the plushie with mock suspicion.

I clutched the bunny to my chest, surprised by how protective I already felt. "Maybe. This one doesn't steal all the covers."

His laugh vibrated through the mattress as he pulled me against his chest, bunny and all.

Later, when Kronos had left for a meeting with a client, I carefully placed the bunny on 'my' side of the bed. I told myself it was just to keep it out of the way, but that didn't explain why I found myself back in the bedroom an hour later, absently stroking its soft ears while I read through work emails.

Or why, the next morning when I had to return to my apartment for fresh clothes, I caught myself reaching for the stupid thing. I'd never admit it to Kronos, but each time I came home, I looked for that splash of cream-colored fur against my sheets, and something in me settled at the sight of it—like some part of him now belonged in my space.

Chapter Thirteen

Glass Deep

Leather & Lace looked nothing like the seedy adult shops that used to pepper the red-light district. The Victorian storefront was all elegant carved wood and frosted glass, display windows arranged with silk robes and crystal bottles that caught the afternoon light. Still, my feet refused to move from the sidewalk.

"Breathe," Kronos murmured, his hand warm at the small of my back. "It's just a store."

"A very expensive store," I said, eyeing the hand-tooled leather pieces in the window. As a craftsman, I could tell the quality—and the probable price tag. "And a very...specific kind of store."

His smile held that predatory edge I was learning to crave. "Consider it a birthday present. Anything you want." His lips brushed my ear. "Tonight, we'll put it to good use."

My skin prickled at his words, remembering how his hands had felt in my shower two weeks ago, how he'd dropped to his knees and taken me apart with ruthless precision. Since the pottery night, something had shifted between us. The texts we'd exchanged this morning were full of promises about making my birthday memorable. However, walking into a high-end sex shop, picking something out...It was mortifying.

"What if someone sees me?" I whispered, though the street was quiet. Old habits died hard—the need to be discrete, to keep my proclivities hidden.

Kronos laughed, his breath warm against my neck. "Half the city's supernatural population shops here. Including some very prominent names who'd rather not have their preferences known. Why do you think the windows are frosted?"

As if to prove his point, the door opened and a woman who could only be a vampire glided out, carrying a discreet black shopping bag. She nodded to Kronos with clear recognition before disappearing into a waiting car.

"See? Perfectly respectable." His hand slid lower on my back, fingers brushing just above the waistband of my jeans in a way that made my breath catch. "Besides, I want to watch you choose. I'd love to see what catches your eye."

The bell above the door chimed as we entered. The interior was even more elegant than the windows suggested—dark wood shelving, plush carpets, and intimate lighting that made everything feel private and luxurious. The air held the rich scent of leather and something spicy, almost like incense but subtler. Soft classical music played just below conversation level, creating a cocoon of privacy around each display. *"¡Ay, Dios!"* I muttered under my breath as I took in the displays.

The toys...were everywhere. Glass cases displayed items that looked more like art pieces than sex accessories. I tried to keep my expression neutral, but my pulse hammered in my throat, making it hard to swallow.

The sales associate who approached us looked like she'd stepped out of a vintage fashion magazine—perfectly coiffed silver hair, elegant black dress, and a pearl choker that wasn't just jewelry, given the faint magical shimmer around it.

"Kronos," she smiled warmly. "It's been too long." Her eyes shifted to me with obvious interest. "And this must be your new friend."

I fought the urge to hide behind him, especially when her gaze lingered on the fading marks visible above my collar—remnants of his mouth from three nights ago. Kronos's hand squeezed my hip reassuringly.

"Celeste, this is Alex. We're here for his birthday gift." His voice carried that note of authority that made my knees weak. "Something special."

"Of course." Her smile turned knowing. "Any particular interests? We just received a lovely collection of Fae-crafted silk ropes..."

The mention of rope sent a jolt of heat straight through me, remembering Kronos's explanation of why he called me rope bunny, how his eyes had darkened as he looked at my bound wrists over dinner.

"Actually," Kronos interrupted, "I'd like Alex to explore first."

"As you wish." She gestured to the various sections of the store. "Take your time. Everything is arranged by category—impact play to the left, restraints along the back wall, sensation toys in the cases…"

The store seemed to go on forever, each section more elaborate than the last. Display cases held items made from materials I'd never seen before—opalescent glass that shifted colors, leather that almost looked alive, silks that shimmered with obvious enchantment.

My fingers trailed over a display of floggers, the soft leather tails caressing my skin. A memory flashed—Kronos's fingernails dragging down my back, the exquisite line between pleasure and pain.

"See anything you'd like to try?" Kronos asked softly, staying close but letting me lead. His presence was both reassuring and nerve-wracking as I moved through the aisles. I glanced back to find his silver eyes tracking my every movement, pupils dilated with interest.

I paused at a case of sensation toys, drawn to something that looked like a feather made of liquid starlight. The price tag made me wince. "These are…"

"Price isn't a concern," he reminded me, his chest brushing my back as he leaned closer. I could feel the steady beat of his heart against my shoulder blade, a stark contrast to my racing pulse. "Tonight is about what you want. If you don't find anything, that's okay and we can find other ways to entertain ourselves."

His breath against my ear made my skin prickle with goosebumps. Two customers passed nearby, their hushed conversation barely registering as Kronos's hand settled at the small of my back again, guiding me deeper into the store.

I spotted a section labeled "Trust Play" tucked away near the back of the store. A blindfold caught my eye—black silk that looked so soft I could almost feel it against my skin. Kronos's texts flashed through my mind—how he'd tie me down, blindfold me, and work me over until I was begging to cum.

My mouth went dry as I reached out, fingers brushing the silk. The material was even softer than it looked, sliding through my fingers like water. I imagined darkness, heightened sensation, Kronos's voice guiding me through pleasure I couldn't anticipate or prepare for.

What really stopped me in my tracks was a sleek black display case. Inside sat a glass prostate massager, deep blue and curved for maximum pressure. The product card promised intense, full-body orgasms and came with a remote control for "external operation." My cock twitched in my jeans at the thought of Kronos controlling it while I was tied up and blindfolded.

I leaned closer to the case, drawn by the way light refracted through the deep blue glass like it was capturing and transforming it. I could almost feel the cool, smooth surface sliding inside me, could imagine Kronos's expression as he watched me take it.

My nervousness must have been more obvious than I thought. I felt the familiar warm tingle at my fingertips and looked down in horror to see tiny blue orbs of light dancing around my hands. I clenched my fist, extinguishing them, but not before Kronos noticed.

"How adorable," he murmured against my ear, his chest pressed to my back. "I've noticed those little lights when you're...excited."

Heat rushed to my ears. "I don't know what you're talking about," I muttered, mortified that he'd recognized my unconscious magical response to being flustered.

"Find something interesting?" Kronos's voice was low in my ear, his chest pressed against my back. His cologne—cedar and something wilder—enveloped me, familiar now after waking up in his bed several times these past weeks.

"I..." The price tag read $1,250, but that wasn't what made me hesitate. It was admitting I wanted him to fuck me with it, to own me completely. "Maybe."

He leaned closer to read the description, his breath warm against my neck. "Excellent choice," he murmured. "Though I'm not surprised. You did seem to enjoy my fingers inside you last time."

My knees weakened at the memory—his fingers stretching me open, finding that spot that had made me cum harder than I ever had before. I'd been face-down in his sheets, biting the pillow to keep from making embarrassing sounds as he worked me open with torturous patience. This toy would take that to an entirely different level.

My face burned at the memory. "It's too much," I protested weakly.

"It's your birthday." His hand settled on my hip, thumb finding the sliver of skin exposed where my shirt had ridden up. The simple skin-to-skin contact made me shiver. "And I want to make it memorable."

His eyes met mine, silver darkening to gunmetal, and I saw the promise there—how he'd use this on me, how he'd take me apart piece by piece and put me back together. The intensity of his gaze made my breath catch.

"Celeste," Kronos called, and she materialized beside us as if by magic. "We'll take this one." His thumb traced circles on my hip as she unlocked the case, my embarrassment warring with anticipation.

She removed the toy, placing it on a velvet cloth. The glass caught the light, sending blue reflections dancing across Kronos's face as he studied it with obvious approval. I couldn't stop staring at his hands as he picked it up, his long fingers wrapping around it in a way that made my stomach clench with want.

She explained its features in such clinical terms that it almost—almost—felt less mortifying. Until she got to the part about different settings, and Kronos's low hum of approval made my stomach flip.

"Would you like it gift wrapped?" she asked with a knowing smile.

"That won't be necessary," Kronos replied, his voice dropping to that register that always made heat pool low in my belly. "We won't be waiting that long to use it."

The discrete black bag she handed us might as well have been transparent for how exposed I felt carrying it. Kronos's hand never left my lower back as we exited the shop.

The cold February air hit me like a shock after the warmth of the store, bringing me back to myself. Then Kronos's lips found the sensitive spot below my ear, and reality blurred again.

"Now," he said as we reached his motorcycle, "what do you say we head home and start your birthday celebration properly?"

"You can't say things like that when we're about to get on your bike," I muttered, already uncomfortably hard in my jeans. The weight of the black bag making it impossible to think of anything but what was coming.

His laugh was rich and dark. "Can't I?" He pressed the bag into my hands before swinging onto the motorcycle. "Hold on tight, and try not to squirm too much."

"*¡Ay yo, Papi!*" I muttered under my breath, rolling my eyes at his teasing.

Kronos paused, one eyebrow raised as he looked back at me. "What did you just call me?"

Heat flooded my face as I realized how it must have sounded to him. "No—it's not—it's just an expression!" I stammered. "It's something Puerto Ricans say when we're exasperated. Like 'oh my god' or 'give me strength.'"

His slow, predatory smile made my stomach flip. "Is that so? Because I rather liked it." He leaned closer, voice dropping to that register that always made my knees weak. "Feel free to call me that again later, when we're putting your birthday gift to use."

I groaned, mortified and aroused in equal measure. "You're impossible."

The ride back to his brownstone felt endless. Every turn, every slight acceleration pressed me against his back, my arms wrapped around his waist. He took one hand off the handlebars at a stoplight, covering mine where it rested on his stomach, guiding it just lower before returning to driving. The casual touch, the implied promise, made my breath catch.

Kronos took the long way home, hitting every bump in the cobblestone streets. Each jolt sent friction through my already sensitive body. By the time we pulled up to his building, I was practically vibrating.

"You're trembling," he observed, voice low as he helped me off the bike. His fingers lingered on my hips, steadying me, though he was the reason I was unsteady in the first place.

"Cold," I lied.

His knowing smirk told me he wasn't fooled. "We should get you inside, then. Warm you up properly."

When we pulled up to his building, my legs were shaky for reasons that had nothing to do with the ride. He caught me as I dismounted, pulling me close.

"Eager?" he asked softly.

"Maybe a lot," I admitted, clutching the bag tighter. The way his eyes darkened made heat pool in my stomach.

"Then let's not waste any more time," he murmured, leading me toward the door.

He led me up to his apartment, that predatory grace making each step feel charged with anticipation. When we entered, I stopped short. The coffee table held a crystal bowl filled with what looked like handmade marshmallows—tiny, perfect cubes dusted with something that sparkled.

"You made these?" I asked, distracted by the weight of the black bag in my hand. I thought about the night in his kitchen when he'd cooked for me, when I'd first admitted my aversion to marshmallows. He'd remembered.

"Mmhm." He picked one up, holding it to my lips. "Rosewater and vanilla bean. Thought it was time to change your opinion about certain textures."

The marshmallow melted on my tongue—nothing like the store-bought kind I hated. This was pure silk, subtle floral notes mixed with rich vanilla. "Oh," I breathed.

"See?" His thumb brushed sugar from my lower lip, lingering there as our eyes locked. "Some things that seem intimidating at first…" His eyes flicked to the bag I was still clutching, "can be exactly what you want." He pressed another marshmallow to my lips. "Better than expected?" His voice held that darkly playful note that made my skin prickle with anticipation.

"Maybe you're right about trying new things," I admitted, heat crawling up my neck as he traced the black bag with his free hand.

"Speaking of…" He guided me to lie back on the couch, his weight settling over me in a way that made my breath catch. "Let me show you how sweet surrender can be."

His fingers worked the buttons of my shirt open with deliberate slowness. The next marshmallow traced a path that made me shiver, leaving trails of sparkling sugar on my skin. I arched into the touch, the memory of clay-covered fingers and shower-slick skin making my head spin with want.

"Happy birthday, little bunny," he murmured against my throat. As he touched me, something broke free from deep inside—blue light spilling from my skin like luminescent petals caught in an invisible breeze. The tiny wisps multiplied with each caress, filling the space between us with my own personal galaxy. I caught Kronos's expression in the azure glow, his silver eyes widening with wonder, reflecting constellations of my creation. I couldn't contain it anymore—didn't want to. For the first time, I let someone witness this most intimate part of me, let my light dance unrestrained around us both.

Each mote pulsed in rhythm with my racing heart, brightening with every touch. The reverence in Kronos's face as he watched my magic embrace us both stole my breath—no one had ever looked at my power that way, like it was something precious rather than useful. His fingers traced through a cluster of lights hovering above my chest, and the wisps followed his movement, as if recognizing him as their own. The room transformed into our private universe, my unrestrained self illuminating the truth I'd been afraid to see for so long.

164

Chapter Fourteen

MARSHMALLOWS

"Stay still," he commanded, surveying my body like an artist considering his canvas. I froze under his molten gaze. The tiny marshmallows glittered between his fingers, each one a delicious threat. His other hand traced the path they would follow, fingertips grazing my skin, leaving goosebumps in their wake.

The first cube settled against my throat, right where my pulse hammered beneath my skin. The sugar was cool and rough. When he placed the second in the hollow of my collarbone, I could already feel it softening, tiny crystals of sugar catching the amber light from his art déco sconces. Over my right nipple, the sensation made me bite my lip hard enough to taste copper. Down my ribs, where my breath caught with each touch, the muscles clenching under his fingers. Into my navel, where the sparkles looked like fallen stars against my skin, the sugar granules tickling sensitive flesh.

His fingers found my jeans, working them open with maddening precision. I wanted to lift my hips, to help, to feel his hands on me, but his earlier command—*stay still*—echoed in my mind. The final marshmallow left a trail of glittering sugar along my hipbone and down toward my cock, which strained painfully against my boxer briefs. The leather creaked under my white-knuckled grip as I fought to remain motionless.

"Look at you," he breathed, drinking in the sight of his work. His pupils had expanded until only a thin ring of silver remained. "Sweet enough to devour."

The word *devour* sent electricity racing through my nerves. I wasn't just prey in that moment—I was a feast laid out specifically for him, decorated and prepared for his pleasure.

Then his mouth found my throat, tongue collecting sugar with devastating thoroughness. The slick heat of it made me suck in a wet, trembling breath, my head falling back to give him better access. Each lick was different—some quick and teasing, barely there before moving on. Others were slow and thorough, his tongue flat and hot against my sensitive skin, keeping me guessing, keeping me trembling. By the time he reached my collarbone, coherent thought was becoming impossible, my world narrowing to the feel of his mouth, the scratch of his stubble, and the points of sugar melting between us.

His tongue traced down my chest, each movement a study in precision. The sugar crystals dissolved under his attention, leaving trails of tingling sensitivity in their wake. He alternated between long, torturous licks that made my muscles clench and quick, teasing flicks that drew helpless sounds from my throat. The slight roughness of his tongue against my nipple had me arching off the couch, forgetting his command.

"I said," he growled, one large hand pressing firmly on my sternum, pinning me down, "stay still."

The reprimand shouldn't have turned me on, but it did. I tried to force my body to obey, though every nerve ending was on fire. His hands tightened on my ribs in response, holding me still for his attention, fingers digging in just enough to leave marks. The thought of carrying his fingerprints on my skin like a brand made my head spin.

"Patience," he crooned against my skin, his breath cooling the wet paths he'd left, sending shivers racing across my heated flesh. The vibration of his voice rumbled through my ribcage, settling low in my gut like liquid heat. "I plan to taste every last crystal." His tongue dipped into my navel with devastating thoroughness, collecting the starlit sugar while his grip kept my hips from bucking upward into the contact I desperately needed. The sound that escaped me wasn't entirely human—half whimper, half growl of frustration.

He took his time with the final marshmallow, the one that had left its trail dangerously close to where I ached for him. His thumbs pressed into my hip bones to keep me pinned as he let me feel every deliberate stroke of his tongue, every careful scrape of teeth. Each time he moved lower, I held my breath, only to have him retreat, teasing, tormenting, never quite where I needed him most.

By the time he finished, I was shaking. Every nerve ending lit up and desperate for more than just teasing touches. The leather cushions creaked under my grip, my nails digging half-moons into the expensive material. *"Por favor,"* I gasped. *"Necesito más…"* Pre-cum had soaked through my boxers, making a visible damp spot that his eyes kept returning to with predatory interest.

"Now," he said, reaching for the black bag with sugar-glazed lips curved in a smile that promised beautiful violence, "should we see what other sweet sounds I can draw from you?"

The toy looked different out of its display box–deep blue glass catching the low light like some ancient magical artifact. The way it curved, how the light bent through it, made it look alive somehow, more real and immediate than it had been in the store's display case. My breath caught in my throat just looking at it, imagining how it would feel inside me, how the smooth, unyielding glass would press against places that would make me forget my name.

Kronos handled it with the same precise care he'd shown with the marshmallows, turning it over in his hands as he explained settings and features. His voice was steady, professional almost, a stark contrast to the hunger in his eyes and the way his cock strained against his jeans. The patient attention in his voice helped calm my racing pulse, even as his other hand never stopped tracing patterns through the sugar still clinging to my skin.

"We'll start slow," he said, showing me the controls of the remote, his thumb caressing each button as he described its function. "Build up to the more...interesting features." His thumb brushed over a crystal of sugar on my hip, making me shiver. "I want you to feel every sensation, learn what you like best."

The toy hummed to life with a soft vibration that filled the room, the sound alone making me twitch in anticipation. His free hand slid lower, trailing heat in its wake until he reached the waistband of my boxers.

"Lift your hips for me," he commanded softly, his voice like velvet-wrapped steel.

When I obeyed, he rewarded me with another lingering kiss on my sugar-dusted skin, just below my navel. His eyes never left mine as he eased the fabric down and off, leaving me exposed to both the cool air and his hungry gaze. I should have felt vulnerable, maybe even embarrassed, but all I felt was a desperate need for him to touch me, to stop teasing and just take what we both wanted.

"Perfect. Now relax and let me show you exactly what this beautiful toy can do."

The glass was cool as he pressed it against my entrance, slick with lube I hadn't even seen him apply. My muscles clenched at the foreign sensation, body tensing against the intrusion despite my eagerness.

"Breathe," Kronos murmured, his free hand stroking along my inner thigh. "Just breathe for me."

His fingers paused, the pressure of the toy steady but not advancing. I forced air into my lungs, trying to focus on his touch rather than the unfamiliar stretch. The first breach sent a jolt through my system—not pain exactly, just intense awareness. My body conflicted between rejecting the intrusion and wanting more.

"That's it," he praised as I exhaled, feeling my muscles yield. "Your body knows what it wants. Listen to it."

He worked the toy in with maddening patience, a fraction of an inch at a time, retreating slightly when I tensed, advancing when I relaxed. Each tiny movement sent new sensations cascading through me—the unyielding hardness of the glass, the perfect curve designed to find spots I hadn't known existed, the cool smoothness warming against my heated skin.

"God," I gasped as the widest part slipped past the tight ring of muscle. My body accepting rather than fighting the intrusion. The change was immediate—discomfort melting into a fullness that bordered on revelation.

Kronos watched my face with laser focus, cataloging every micro-expression. "There we go," he said, voice rough with approval. "Your body's learning."

"I can take more than that," I managed, though my voice shook as his fingers traced teasing patterns along my inner thigh, never quite reaching where I wanted them.

His laugh was dark and rich, vibrating through me where his chest pressed against my leg. "Oh, I know you can, little bunny. But I want to watch you fall apart." He nipped at my hip, soothing the sting with his tongue. "I want to see every reaction, hear every sound, and feel you tremble for me. I need to know exactly how to wreck you."

The last words were almost a growl, sending a fresh wave of heat through me. This wasn't just about pleasure—it was about claiming, about marking me from the inside out.

The first plunge of the toy inside made me gasp—even before he turned it on, the smooth glass was overwhelming, the curve of it pressing places that made lights dance behind my eyes. Kronos kept his movements torturously slow.

"Beautiful," he cooed, adjusting the angle.

Then he clicked the first setting, and my world exploded. The vibration started gentle but still drew a sound from my throat I'd never heard myself make—something between a gasp and a moan that pleased him, judging by the darkening of his eyes.

"That's it. Let me hear you." He played my body like an instrument he'd mastered years ago, knowing when to increase intensity, when to back off, when to add that maddening rotating feature that made stars burst behind my eyes. The pressure built in waves, receding just before cresting, keeping me suspended in a state of desperate need.

"Please," I gasped, not even sure what I was begging for—release? Mercy? More? My hands clawed at the leather cushions as he found yet another pattern that made coherent thought impossible, the glass toy brushing my prostate with unerring accuracy.

"Not yet," he purred, free hand sliding up to pinch my nipple, adding a sharp counterpoint to the deep, pulsing pleasure inside me. "I'm nowhere near done with you."

Just when I thought I couldn't take anymore, he clicked another button. The thrusting motion combined with everything else had me crying out his name, back arching so hard it almost hurt. My whole body shook as pleasure built to impossible heights, every muscle straining toward a release he kept just out of reach.

His touch was both possessive and reverent, like he couldn't get enough of watching me come undone beneath him. His eyes gleamed in the low light, tracking every twitch, every gasp, every aborted thrust of my hips.

"You're doing so good," he breathed, adjusting the angle again, so the glass pressed even more firmly against that spot inside me that made my vision blur. "So responsive for me." When he clicked to the next setting, combining thrusting with that maddening rotation, my back arched off the couch, a broken moan tearing from my throat. His name became a prayer, a plea, the only word I remembered how to say.

"Look at me," he commanded. It took an enormous effort to focus, to drag my eyes open and meet his. When I managed it, his eyes were blazing with that predatory hunger, pupils so dilated they swallowed the silver. His face was flushed with arousal, lips parted, breath coming faster than usual. The knowledge that watching me like this affected him so deeply pushed me even closer to the edge.

Release hit like lightning, pulses radiating outward from where the toy pressed inside me, through every inch of my body. My vision whited out, muscles seizing as I came harder than I ever had in my life, untouched, just from the toy and his hands and the heat of his gaze. Through the haze of ecstasy, I felt his hands steadying me, heard his voice praising me, anchoring me as wave after wave of bliss crashed through my system.

When I could remember how to breathe, he was gathering me against his chest, one arm supporting my shoulders while the other carefully removed the toy. His heartbeat thundered under my ear as he stroked my back, pressing soft kisses to my temple, my cheekbone, the corner of my mouth. My entire body felt liquid, boneless, as if all my muscles had dissolved under the onslaught of pleasure.

"You did such a good job." I could hear the smile in his voice. He let me catch my breath for a few moments. Though my body was spent, I could feel his arousal pressed against me, reminding me he hadn't found his own release yet. The knowledge sent a pleasant shiver through me, despite my exhaustion.

"Think you need a moment?" he asked, his voice gentle but tinged with that hunger I was coming to crave, the edge that reminded me what he was, what he wanted from me.

"I'm good," I replied, surprising myself with how much I meant it. My body might be wrung out, but I wanted to taste him, wanted to feel him lose control the way I just had. "What did you have in mind?"

He shifted, reaching for something beside the couch. The soft whisper of rope against leather made my pulse quicken again - the purple silk rope from the dining experience. This time, his expression promised something more intense.

"Think you can handle more?" he asked, the purple rope sliding through his fingers like liquid shadow. "I'd like to try something a bit more complex this time."

He paused, studying my face with careful attention. Something in my expression must have shown my fatigue, because his demeanor shifted.

"Actually, come here." He gathered me into his arms before I could respond, lifting me as if I weighed nothing at all.

"I can walk," I protested, though my legs still felt like jelly, muscles trembling with aftershocks every few seconds.

"Mmm, but I enjoy carrying you." He pressed a kiss to my temple as he headed for his bedroom, navigating the doorways with practiced ease despite his burden. "Besides, I want you comfortable with what comes next. The bed will be better for rope work than the couch."

His massive four-poster loomed before us, sheets turned down as if he'd prepared for this hours ago. He laid me on the Egyptian cotton with surprising gentleness for someone who'd just spent the last hour driving me crazy.

"Now," he said, the rope catching the soft light as he moved to join me, kneeling beside me on the mattress.

"Let's try something a little more elaborate than last time. Hands in front of you, bunny."

The mattress dipped under his weight, the familiar scent of him—cedar and storm and something wilder—enveloping me as he leaned closer.

The rope wound around my wrists as Kronos worked, each loop carefully placed for my comfort. His touch remained gentle but deliberate, checking the tension with care, his fingers slipping beneath the bindings to ensure they weren't too tight. Unlike our first rope experience, where he'd bound my wrists while feeding me, this pattern created an intricate web that was both decorative and functional.

"This is a modified box tie," he explained, his voice taking on that instructional tone. "It will keep your arms secure but comfortable while still allowing some movement."

I watched, fascinated, as he worked his way up my forearms, creating diamond patterns with the purple silk that contrasted against my skin. The methodical process was almost hypnotic—the soft sound of rope sliding through his hands, the gentle pressure as he adjusted each section, the quiet concentration on his face. I relaxed into his expert handling, surrendering to his care in a way that would have terrified me weeks ago.

"Good?" he asked, fingers trailing over the finished work. I nodded, testing the bindings by flexing my arms. They held secure but not tight, leaving enough room for circulation while displaying my arms in what felt like an artistic arrangement, something to be admired.

"You are breathtaking, my love," he cooed, his eyes darkening as he took in the full effect of his work—me sprawled on his bed, arms bound in intricate patterns, skin still flushed from orgasm and marked with fading sugar crystals. "Now, I want to feel that perfect mouth of yours."

He guided me to kneel on the bed, arranging my bound arms in front of me so I could balance. The position emphasized how the ropes framed my upper body, making me aware of my vulnerability.

When he positioned himself in front of me, his jeans discarded. Heat flooded through me all over again. The sight of him—powerful thighs, taut abdomen, cock hard with a bead of pre-cum already gathered at the tip—made my mouth water. The first taste of him made my head spin.

His fingers twisted in my hair, grip tightening as he took control. Instead of letting me set the pace, he thrust forward, filling my mouth in one smooth movement that made my eyes water.

"Take it deeper," he growled, the command sending shivers down my spine. "I know you can."

He pushed again, cock hitting the back of my throat. I gagged, unprepared for the depth, throat convulsing around him. My eyes watered, vision blurring as my body fought between the need for air and the desire to please him.

"Relax," he instructed, not withdrawing despite my struggle. "Breathe through your nose. You can take all of me." His grip held me firmly in place, leaving no room for retreat. I forced my throat to relax, focused on pulling air through my nose in desperate little snatches. My head swam, oxygen-deprivation making the edges of my vision darken.

Just when spots began dancing across my sight, he pulled back—not fully, just enough to let me gulp a partial breath before he thrust deep again. This time I was more prepared, throat opening to accommodate him as he sank impossibly deeper.

"Perfect," he praised, voice ragged with pleasure. "Look at you, taking my cock so beautifully."

Pride surged through me despite—or perhaps because of—the ache in my jaw and the burn in my lungs. His hips began a rhythm that left me on the edge of breathlessness, pulling back just enough to prevent me from passing out before driving deep again. Each thrust pushed my limits further, training my body to accept him, to want him deeper.

A deep groan ripped from his throat as I hollowed my cheeks, the vibration of it buzzing through his cock and onto my tongue. When I swallowed around his tip, he hissed, hips jerking forward. The sound shot straight to my dick, which twitched against all logic, filling again, though I'd already cum twice. My jaw ached, stretched to its limit around his girth. My scalp burned where his fingers twisted in my hair. My knees dug into the mattress, pain flaring with each tiny shift.

He thrust again, cock hitting the back of my throat. I gagged, eyes watering, throat convulsing around him. Couldn't breathe. My lungs seized, panic flaring for a split second before his grunt of pleasure drowned everything else out. The rope bit into my wrists when I tried to pull back. His grip tightened in my hair, holding me firmly in place as black spots danced in my vision. My chest screamed for air, cock throbbing painfully in counterpoint to my racing pulse. Just when darkness started closing in, he pulled back—just enough for me to drag in half a breath through my nose before he pushed in again, somehow deeper than before.

The slick, obscene noises of my mouth stretched around him, of spit running down my chin, filled the room along with his ragged breathing. His thrusts grew faster, more desperate, his composure cracking with each movement. His fingers twisted painfully in my hair, holding me exactly where he wanted me.

"Fuck, fuck, fuck," he growled, voice barely human. "I'm going to cum, bunny."

His cock swelled against my tongue, pulsing hard before the first hot burst hit the back of my throat. I swallowed, surprised that it still tasted like candy apples. How the hell did he do that? Another pulse, stronger than the first. His grip held me in place, ensuring I couldn't pull back even if I'd wanted to.

"That's it," he groaned, hips jerking forward with each wave. "Swallow all of it. Every. Last. Drop."

I gulped desperately, the sweetness flooding my mouth, overwhelming my senses. *What the fuck? Why did he taste so good?*

His body shuddered above me, muscles tensing and releasing as he emptied himself down my throat. When he pulled back enough for me to breathe, my head spun from oxygen deprivation and the lingering sweetness on my tongue.

Time blurred. His grip gentled in my hair, stroking rather than pulling. My jaw ached as he withdrew, thumb catching a string of saliva and cum from my swollen lips. My body felt disconnected, floating in the aftermath of submission.

Strong arms lifted and arranged me against solid warmth. I collapsed against him, boneless and dazed, the rope around my wrists suddenly gone, though I hadn't felt him remove it. The world narrowed to his heartbeat under my cheek, his scent filling my lungs as I gulped air.

"Fuck," he groaned, his voice a warm rumble against my ear. "You did so fucking well for me."

He cradled me close while my breathing steadied, one hand running through my hair, working out tangles with careful fingers. After a few moments, he shifted to examine my wrists where the rope had been, pressing gentle kisses to the faint marks left behind, the sensitive skin tingling under his attention.

"How do your shoulders feel?" he asked, fingers finding and working through any tension the position might have left, his touch both clinical and intimate. I hummed, too blissed out for words, floating in the peaceful aftermath. His warmth and the soft sheets were pulling me toward sleep, but I fought to stay awake, wanting to savor this moment—the safety of his arms, the tenderness that was so at odds with the wolf I knew lurked beneath the surface.

"Rest," he murmured, tucking the blanket around us both, his body curled around mine. "I've got you."

"Thank you," I said, as I let my eyes drift closed. The last thought before sleep claimed me was how strangely perfect this was—me, bound and pliant in the loving arms of this wondrous man, feeling safer than I ever had before.

Chapter Fifteen

Comeuppance

Kronos's kiss still lingered on my lips as I shuffled through his kitchen, mentally cataloging what I needed for tonight's dinner. This morning, he'd pressed me against the bedroom doorframe, hair still damp from the shower, his body radiating that supernatural warmth that always made me want to lean into him like a cat seeking sunshine.

"I'll be late," he'd chuckled against my mouth. "I'm meeting with the police about that bail jumper."

I'd nodded, fingers tangling in his shirt to pull him back for one more kiss. "Are you going to tell me how you tracked him across three state lines in two days?"

His laugh had rumbled through both of us. "That's a trade secret." I melted as his tongue swirled the tip of my ear, catching the tip between his teeth. "Don't wait up if I'm really late." *As if I'd let him leave now.*

"I might have plans for you," I'd countered.

"Hmm?"

"Dinner. Here. I'm cooking." I said with a smile, tapping him on the nose. I had to get going, or I'd never make it before the store closed. I wished everything wouldn't close early on Mondays, but that's southern towns for you.

Something surprised and pleased had flickered across his face. "Are you now?" His kiss had deepened, plunging his tongue in and caressing the roof of my mouth and tongue. I would not let him leave. "Then I'll definitely be home by seven."

I pouted as he pulled back and slipped out of my arms. He'd left soon after, promising to text me when he got there and when he left so I'd be ready for him. I never asked him to do that…but I loved that he did.

Now, six hours later, I was actually going through with it. My cooking skills were barely passable, but even I could handle steaks, baked potatoes, and a simple salad. Something that wouldn't embarrass me too badly compared to his gourmet meals, but would still show…what? That I cared? That I was trying?

The thought made my stomach flutter in a way that was becoming distressingly familiar. Over the past week, I'd practically lived at his place, only returning to my apartment above Twyla's shop to grab fresh clothes or work on custom orders. The transition had been so smooth, so natural, that I hadn't noticed until this morning when I realized I knew exactly where everything in his kitchen was kept.

"Boyfriend" seemed too juvenile a word for what Kronos was becoming to me. "Partner" felt too formal, too much like a business arrangement. Whatever we were, it had grown roots I hadn't noticed planting.

I checked the shopping list on my phone again. Kronos had texted that he'd be home by seven after tracking down some bail jumper who'd tried skipping town. That gave me plenty of time to get what I needed and still prepare dinner before he arrived.

The butcher shop two blocks from his brownstone was my first stop—a place Kronos swore by for its locally sourced meats. The bell jingled as I pushed open the door, the familiar scent of sawdust and fresh meat greeting me.

"Well, if it isn't the hunter's shadow," the old butcher called from behind the counter. His weathered face creased into a smile as I approached. The first time I'd come in, he'd taken one look at me and asked if I was "Orestes's new pup." I still wasn't sure if that was a comment on our relationship or something more, knowing about Kronos's nature.

"Two ribeye's, please," I said, trying not to flush at the knowing gleam in his eye. "The thicker cut, if you have it."

He nodded approvingly. "Special occasion?"

I shrugged, aiming for casual. "Just dinner."

"Mmhmm." His smile widened as he selected two perfect steaks from the display. "First time cooking for him, eh? Don't worry, these beauties are so good you'd have to really try to mess 'em up."

I didn't have to try. I had a habit of nearly burning down my apartment whenever I tried to cook. Twyla refused to replace my oven again. "That obvious, huh?"

"Son, I've been married forty-two years." He wrapped the steaks in butcher paper with practiced movements. "I know that look. The 'I want to do something nice but I'm scared I'll screw it up' look."

I anxiously rubbed the back of my neck, shrugging in embarrassment. My gaze dropped to the floor, then darted around the room—anywhere but at their face. "Yeah, well...I'm not exactly a chef," I mumbled, the words tumbling out too quickly and slightly too loud, followed by a stiff, uncomfortable laugh that died as soon as it escaped.

"Doesn't matter." He handed me the package with a wink. "Man, like Orestes? It's the thought that counts. Though..." he leaned in conspiratorially, "a pinch of this wouldn't hurt." He slid a small container of seasoning across the counter. "On the house."

The market for produce was next. I selected potatoes that looked about the right size for baking, running through the steps Kronos had shown me the last time we'd cooked together. Remembering his hands over mine, showing me how to check if something was done properly, made my chest feel tight in a way that was becoming familiar.

My phone buzzed as I was paying for the vegetables.

Twyla: *Mira and I are going 2 try 2 C if we can get into that art exhibit tonight! E. Thalassos was rumored to have donated one of his paintings!! I'm so excited!*

Something uncomfortable curled in my stomach. E. Thalassos, the siren she'd found on social media a few months ago. He had flowing pastel pink hair and a voice that made everyone within earshot hang on his every word. I'd only met him once, and hadn't liked how fake he was. Something about him made me feel…unsettled.

Me: *Be careful. Remember what I told you about sirens?*

I trusted Twyla's judgment, mostly. But sirens had reputations not unlike mermaids—beautiful, seductive, and with a nasty habit of luring unwary victims to watery graves. At least, that's what the stories said. I wasn't sure how much was fact versus fiction, but it made me concerned.

Twyla: *OMFG ur such a worrier! Sirens haven't drowned anybody in CENTURIES. It's literally illegal now. You stress 2 much!*

As if it wasn't always illegal to kill and eat people. I grimaced, remembering my first and only encounter with Ezra three weeks ago. It was his voice that had set me on edge. When he'd spoken, the sound had seemed to bypass my ears and vibrate directly through my bones.

I'd watched with growing unease as everyone, including the men, had practically melted listening to him.

Me: *Humor me. Text the code word in 2 hours?*

Our safety system—a random word we changed weekly that meant "I'm safe" when texted unprompted. This week it was "sunshine."

Twyla: *Fine, MOM. But only becuz u'd just worry urself sick otherwise.*
Twyla: *BTW how are things with Mr. Tall, Dangerous & Sexy? Have you admitted he's your BOYFRIEND yet?*

I rolled my eyes, but couldn't suppress a smile.

Alex: *Focus on your own love life. I'll let you know if there's anything to tell.*
Twyla: *There already IS and you know it! K gotta go beautify. TTYL XOXO.*

I was still scowling at my phone, half-amused and half-worried, when the hair on the back of my neck stood up. The street around me felt too quiet. Something in my gut—the same instinct that had kept me alive on the streets—screamed danger.

I turned, groceries clutched against my chest, just as something heavy and dark dropped over my head. Rough fabric scraped my face, smelling of dust and chemicals.

My glamour flared, but whoever had me wasn't human enough to be affected. Strong hands yanked my arms behind my back, the grocery bags tumbling to the sidewalk. Food scattered across concrete as something bound my wrists.

"What the—" My protest was cut short by a hard blow to my stomach that knocked the wind from my lungs. The pain blossomed, radiating outward as I doubled over. I tried to kick out, to fight back, but whoever had me was fast. My foot connected with something solid, earning me a grunt of pain, but the victory was short-lived.

"Shut up," a gravelly voice hissed near my ear, breath hot through the fabric covering my head. "One sound and we slit your throat right here."

The blade pressed against my neck felt cold, the edge sharp enough that even the slightest pressure drew a thin line of warmth that trickled down my collarbone. They weren't bluffing.

I heard a car trunk open, the hydraulics hissing as the lid raised. Panic surged through me as I was manhandled toward it. I thrashed, fighting despite the knife. This would be my last chance before they got me somewhere private. Somewhere no one would hear me scream.

"Hold still, you little shit," a second voice growled, this one deeper, with the distinctive rumble of the Madam's granite-skinned enforcer. His fist connected with my temple, and stars burst behind my eyelids. The world tilted as I was shoved into the trunk, my head cracking against something hard on the way in.

"The Madam sends her regards," the first voice sneered. "Your boyfriend's not around to save you this time, pretty boy."

The trunk slammed shut, plunging me into darkness. The silence was broken only by my ragged breathing and the engine roaring to life. As the car lurched forward, all I could think about was Kronos coming home to an empty apartment, the dinner I'd planned to make scattered on some sidewalk, and the terrifying certainty that the Madam had decided I was too much trouble to keep alive.

Chapter Sixteen

PROMISE

The darkness in the trunk was absolute, broken only by the occasional flash of light through seams when we passed street lamps. Every bump in the road sent fresh waves of pain through my ribs. I struggled against the thick rope binding my wrists, the coarse fibers rubbing my skin raw until something warm trickled down my palms.

I'd been in the trunk for what felt like hours, drifting in and out of consciousness. A vibration against my hip jolted me alert. *My phone.* It was still in my back pocket—I could feel it. Another vibration. Someone was texting me.

With effort, I twisted my body, ignoring the stabbing pain in my side. If I could just reach it... After several agonizing attempts, I contorted enough that my bound hands could graze the edge of my pocket. The phone vibrated again.

I strained further, fingertips catching the fabric. My fingers, already slick with blood or sweat, fumbled with the pocket. When I worked the phone free, it slipped from my hands, clattering somewhere in the trunk's darkness.

"*Mierda*," I hissed, panic rising as I frantically felt around the confined space. "*Vamos. Vamos…*" My shoulders screamed in protest as I stretched, fingers sweeping across the rough carpet lining.

The car hit another pothole, sending the phone sliding against my leg. I trapped it against the floor with my knee, then maneuvered until I could grasp it between my palms.

With trembling hands, I managed to wake the screen. The light was blinding in the darkness, but I squinted through the pain. Unlocking it blind was almost impossible with bound hands. It took three tries before I felt the vibration confirming success. I knew Kronos's contact was the first in my favorites list—one swipe, then tap. I couldn't see if the call connected.

"Kronos," I whispered, unsure if he could hear me over the road noise. "Trunk. Madam. Help." I tried to give more details, but the car turned sharply and the phone slipped from my fingers.

I cursed, desperately trying to find it again in the darkness. The car hit another pothole, and my head slammed against the trunk lid. Stars burst behind my eyelids, and for a moment, everything went fuzzy.

By the time I regained my senses, the car was slowing. Gravel crunched beneath the tires, the surface change vibrating through the metal frame. We were off the main roads then. My fingers found the phone again, but there was no way to know if my message had gotten through.

The engine died. Car doors opened and slammed shut. Heavy footsteps approached the trunk, and my heart hammered painfully against my bruised ribs. I pressed what I hoped was SEND on a final text before light flooded the compartment.

"Look what we found," the gravelly voice said, yanking the phone from my hands. The screen lit his face from below—the shadowy enforcer Smokey, his features half-hidden in perpetual darkness that moved like living ink. "Trying to call for help? Cute."

His fist connected with my temple before I could respond. The world exploded into pain, then nothing at all.

Cold water shocked me back to consciousness, rushing up my nose and making me sputter and choke. The hood was gone, but my vision swam, refusing to focus. When it finally cleared, I found myself in what looked like an abandoned warehouse. Moonlight filtered through broken windows, illuminating rusted machinery and graffiti-covered walls.

My arms were wrenched behind me, the rope digging into my wrists. I was seated on a metal chair that bit into my thighs. The rope was coarse—not the silky bindings Kronos used, but something meant to hurt, to restrain by force rather than consent.

"He's awake." Granite stepped into my line of sight, massive and imposing in the dim light. The crystalline patterns of his skin caught the moonlight, making him look carved from stone. "Finally."

A fist slammed into my face, whipping my head back. Blood filled my mouth, hot and coppery. Another blow caught me in the stomach. Pain splintered through my torso, and I would have doubled over if not for the ropes.

"Stop," I gasped, spitting blood onto the concrete floor. "What do you want?"

He laughed, the sound like rocks grinding together. "Me? I don't want anything." Another punch, this one catching my cheekbone and splitting it open. "I just enjoy hurting you."

Through the ringing in my ears, I tried to focus. "Why? What did I ever do to you?" I coughed, more blood spattering down my shirt. "We rarely spoke when I worked there."

His massive hand gripped my hair, yanking my head back until I was forced to meet his eyes—cold and hard as the crystals embedded in his skin. "You don't get it, do you? Before you came along, I was her favorite."

"The Madam's?" I stared at him in disbelief. She'd never shown him anything but haughty disdain when I was around. I'm not even sure she knew his name.

"Seven years I was her right hand." His grip tightened. "Then she found you, with your pretty face and your charm, and suddenly I'm reduced to bodyguard." He reared back and spit in my face. "You do not know what you threw away. What some of us would kill for?"

Gross, his spit got in my cut. Who knows what that block of rock had in his system? If I made it out of this, I was going to need shots. "Why would anyone want that kind of attention from her? She's a monster."

The back of his hand cracked across my face so hard I tasted fresh blood. "Not everyone thinks of this as a bad life," he snarled. "Most of us chose it. Were happy there. Content."

"You chose to be her puppet?" I couldn't keep the disbelief from my voice.

"At least it's honest work." His eyes burned with something that looked almost like religious fervor. "The most honest way there is to make a living. You give pleasure, you get paid. Simple." His expression darkened. "But you treated it like a punishment. Like something shameful. Paraded around like you were better than the rest of us."

"I'm sorry," I said, meaning it despite everything. "I didn't realize."

"Of course you didn't." He stepped back, brushing imaginary dust from his knuckles. "Too busy playing victim when the rest of us were just doing our jobs."

I swallowed more blood, wincing at the raw feeling in my throat. "This isn't what I'd have chosen for myself if I'd had a choice. And I've moved on now." I looked up at him, trying for sincerity despite my battered face. "Why can't you just let me go?"

"Because no one leaves before their time is up." The Madam's voice sliced through the warehouse like a silk-wrapped blade. She sauntered into view, her hot pink dress almost luminous in the darkness. Every movement was calculated seduction, the air around her shimmering with lotus-eater magic. "It sets a terrible example."

While they'd been focused on my face, I'd been working at the ropes binding my wrists. The blood from my earlier cuts made the fibers slick, and I could feel them starting to give. I just needed to keep them talking.

"Michelle," I acknowledged, using her real name instead of her title. A tiny rebellion, but her slight frown showed it hit its mark.

"My darlin' Will-o'-Wisp." Her southern accent thickened as she approached, heels clicking on the concrete floor. "How I've missed you." She trailed manicured fingers down my cheek, her touch burning like acid against my skin. Lotus-eater venom, designed to make humans pliant and addicted. My half-fae blood made me resistant, but it still stung.

"Can't say the feeling's mutual." Another twist of my wrists, the rope giving a little more.

She laughed, the sound like breaking glass. "Always so spirited. That's why you were my favorite." She glanced at Granite, whose expression didn't change, though something tightened around his eyes. "But bad boys who disappoint me have to be punished."

From her clutch purse, she withdrew a document written on what looked suspiciously like human skin; the letters shimmering with a sickly green glow. "You never terminated your contract, darlin'. Seven years of service, and you've barely given me three.

"I don't owe you anything." The rope was loose enough now that I could slip one hand free if I dislocated my thumb. It would hurt like hell, but not as much as whatever she had planned.

"I have witnesses who would disagree." She nodded toward Smokey, who materialized from the shadows, darkness writhing around him like living ink. "Customers who were very disappointed when their favorite performer vanished." She produced a wickedly sharp pin from her hair. "All I need is your signature. In blood, of course. Then you can come back where you belong, earn your keep like a good boy, and everything will be forgiven."

She pressed the pin against my lip, drawing a bead of crimson. "Or we can do this the hard way. Your precious Primal won't find you in time to save you, I'm afraid. My shadow wolves have led him on quite the merry chase through the city." She smiled, revealing very sharp teeth. "By the time he realizes the trail is false, you'll be back on stage where you belong. Blissfully unaware."

"I'd rather die," I spat.

Her smile didn't waver. "That can be arranged too, darlin'. Though it seems like such a waste of that pretty face." She leaned closer, the contract hovering between us. At that moment, I made my decision. With a sharp push, I dislocated my thumb, biting my cheek to keep from screaming as pain shot up my arm. My hand slipped free of the restraints.

The Madam's eyes widened in surprise—the only warning she got before I sprung up from the chair and swung my still-bound hands like a club, connecting with the side of her head with a satisfying crack. She went down hard, the contract fluttering forgotten to the floor. Granite roared in fury, lunging for me, but I was already diving to the side, narrowly avoiding his massive fist as it cracked the concrete where my head had been seconds before.

I scrambled to my feet, still dizzy from blood loss and pain, and ran for the nearest window. Smokey's darkness surged toward me, tendrils of shadow trying to wrap around my ankles. I jumped, crashing through already broken glass, fresh cuts opening across my face and arms.

Landing hard on gravel, I barely had time to register the pain before a hand closed around my ankle. I kicked out blindly, connecting with something solid. There was a grunt of pain, and the grip loosened just enough for me to wrench free.

The forest loomed ahead, dark and forbidding, but it offered cover. I ran, adrenaline numbing the worst of the pain as branches whipped against my already-bloody face. Behind me, I could hear the heavy footfalls of Granite and the whisper-silent movement of Smokey's shadows.

"The wolves," I heard the Madam command from somewhere behind me, her voice tight with fury. "Get the wolves!"

Fear gave my legs new strength as I crashed deeper into the trees. Wolves. Shadow wolves—the most vicious of the shadow realm predators, capable of tearing a man apart in seconds. A howl split the night, too close for comfort. Not an ordinary wolf—the sound was wrong, like glass breaking underwater.

Moonlight broke through the canopy, illuminating a small clearing ahead. I stumbled toward it, hoping for better visibility, for some advantage. Blood dripped from my various cuts, leaving a trail even a novice could follow. For shadow wolves, it might as well have been a neon sign.

The first wolf emerged from the darkness to my left—massive, its body seeming to absorb the moonlight rather than reflect it. Eyes like toxic waste glowed in its skull, and smoke curled from its fur with each movement. Two more materialized on my right, cutting off my escape.

I backed up until my shoulders hit rough bark. Trapped. I'd led myself straight into their perfect hunting ground.

The pack circled slowly, coordinating their approach with the patient certainty of apex predators. My glamour would be ineffective against these creatures. They hunted by instinct, not sight—they could sense the power beneath my skin.

I pressed my back against the rough bark, mind racing through limited options. My usual tricks wouldn't work here. The blue fire that marked me as a will-o'-wisp was something I used sparingly—quick flashes to distract, to redirect attention, to create openings for escape. Never as a weapon.

Unfortunately, I was out of options.

The lead wolf tensed, haunches coiling for the final lunge. I closed my eyes for a moment, reaching for that familiar well of power I usually kept tightly capped. When I opened them again, my fingertips were already tingling with suppressed energy.

"Let's see how you like the light," I muttered, feeling the cool burn of blue fire rising to the surface.

The wolf sprang forward, jaws opening impossibly wide to reveal teeth like polished obsidian. I threw up my hands, releasing the control I normally maintained with such careful precision. Blue flames erupted from my palms—not the gentle, hypnotic wisps I used for distraction, but concentrated streams of cerulean fire that illuminated the clearing in ghostly light.

The wolf yelped as the flames caught it mid-leap, sending it sprawling. The magic burned through its smoky fur, leaving patches that glowed like dying embers. The creature's howl of pain sent shivers down my spine, but I couldn't afford mercy. Not now.

I'd never channeled this much power at once. The sensation was exhilarating and terrifying—like standing in the eye of a storm I wasn't sure I could control.

The remaining wolves hesitated, their toxic-green eyes reflecting my blue fire. They'd expected easy prey, not this. I took advantage of their uncertainty, swinging my arm in a wide arc, trailing blue flames like a whip. It caught one across the muzzle, drawing another glass-shattering howl.

The third wolf's teeth snapped inches from my throat—I barely got my forearm up in time. Its bite sank into flesh, but my magic flared on contact. The creature recoiled, its jaw smoking where it had touched me, shadows burning away to reveal the emptiness beneath.

Blood ran hot down my arm, but adrenaline kept the pain at bay. I called for more power, surprised at how readily it answered—as if it had been waiting for permission to be unleashed. The blue flames danced higher, crawling up my arms in patterns that matched the racing of my pulse.

The wolves circled more cautiously now, wary of the light emanating from my skin. I could feel the strain of maintaining this level of power. My vision tunneled, dark spots dancing at the edges. My knees threatened to buckle. This wasn't sustainable—will-o'-wisps weren't meant to burn this bright for this long.

The largest wolf gathered itself for another attack. I met it with a desperate surge of power that made my vision white out momentarily. The blast caught it square in the chest, and for a moment, it hung suspended in the air. Then, with a sound like thunder imploding, it disintegrated—smoke and shadow collapsing in on itself until nothing remained.

The other wolves attacked as one, sensing my weakening state. I stumbled backward, blue fire flaring from my hands in uncontrolled bursts. One caught a wolf in the throat, leaving a burning hole clean through to the other side. It dissolved like the first, but not before its claws raked down my side.

Pain lanced through me, but I kept the flames flowing, drawing on reserves I rarely accessed. The third wolf leapt, and I threw myself to the side, rolling through undergrowth and coming up bleeding from a dozen fresh cuts. The wolf had overshot, and my next blast caught it from behind. It shattered like black glass, fragments dissolving into nothing before they hit the ground.

I collapsed to my knees, chest heaving, the light flickering and dying around my trembling hands.

Victory was short-lived.

From the shadows between the trees, darkness coalesced into Smokey's human form—or what passed for it. His face contorted with rage as he surveyed the empty clearing where his wolves had been.

"You'll pay for that," he hissed, darkness pouring from his fingers like liquid night. "Those were my favorites."

I tried to summon more light, but I was drained. My arms drooped like lead weights, and when I tried to stand, my legs betrayed me. I'd given everything to defeat the wolves.

The darkness reached me before I could move, wrapping around my throat like a garrote. I clawed at it desperately, fingers passing through a shadow that was solid enough to choke the life from me. Spots danced across my vision, lungs burning for air that wouldn't come.

"I'm going to enjoy watching the light go out in your eyes," Smokey whispered, drawing closer. "Slowly. So you feel every second."

I was going to die here, in the middle of nowhere, without ever seeing Kronos again. I'd never get to tell him what I'd planned…tonight…

A roar split the night—primal, ancient, furious. Something massive crashed through the trees, too fast to track. One moment Smokey was standing over me—the next he was flying backward, slammed into a tree trunk with bone-crushing force.

The shadows around my neck dissolved, and I collapsed, gasping for precious air. Through watering eyes, I saw Kronos silhouetted against the moonlight. Claws extended from his fingers, his teeth too sharp in his mouth, eyes blazing with monstrous rage.

Smokey recovered quickly, darkness gathered around him like armor. "You're too late, wolf. He's already half dead."

"You'll be all dead," Kronos growled, the words barely human, "if you've touched him again."

They collided in a blur of motion too fast to follow—light and darkness, predator and shadow. Trees shuddered under the impact of bodies thrown with inhuman force. The ground trembled. Darkness exploded in tendrils, only to be shredded by claws that gleamed like silver in the moonlight.

I tried to push myself up, to help somehow, but my body refused to cooperate. The best I could manage was to drag myself toward a fallen log, something to put at my back. From this relative safety, I watched Kronos tear through Smokey's defenses with ruthless efficiency.

"You can't kill shadow," Smokey taunted, even as Kronos's claws shredded another tendril of darkness.

When Kronos finally pinned Smokey against an ancient oak, claws pressed to his throat, I thought it was over. Darkness bubbled from the shadow-man's mouth, a last desperate attack. It engulfed Kronos's head, trying to suffocate him as it had me.

"Kronos!" I shouted, the sound tearing painfully from my abused throat.

Something in my voice must have reached him, because he stilled for a split second. Then, with deliberate slowness, he reached up and tore the darkness away like it was nothing more than cobwebs. Smokey's eyes widened in genuine fear.

"Impossible," he whispered.

Kronos smiled. "I've been hunting your kind for years." His voice was almost conversational, which somehow made it more terrifying. "Did you really think a little shadow would stop me?"

The sound of sirens cut through the night, red and blue lights flashing through the trees. Smokey's head whipped toward them, sudden panic replacing his usual cold confidence.

"Police?" He looked genuinely confused. "How—"

"I called them before I came for you," Kronos said, satisfaction clear in his voice. "Right after I got a very interesting text from Alex. They should be arresting the Madam and her friend right about now."

Smokey thrashed in his grip, darkness flaring in one last attempt at escape. Kronos casually slammed him back against the tree, hard enough that I heard something crack. The shadow-man went limp, darkness receding until he looked almost human—just a thin, pale man in expensive clothes, unconscious but still breathing.

Only then did Kronos turn to me, eyes still glowing with predatory light. He crossed the clearing in three strides, dropping to his knees beside me. His hands—human again, claws retracted—hovered over my injuries, unsure where it was safe to touch.

"Alex," he breathed, voice rough with emotion. "What did they do to you?"

I tried to smile, though I suspected it came out as more of a grimace through the blood. "You should see the other guys."

His laugh was shaky, relief mixed with lingering fear. "I did. You took down three shadow wolves on your own." His fingers gently brushed my hair back from my forehead, careful to avoid the worst bruises.

"I'm just as surprised as you," I managed before a coughing fit doubled me over. When I could breathe again, I found myself cradled against his chest, his heartbeat steady under my ear. "Did my message really go through?"

"Trunk. Madam. Help," he quoted. "Not your most eloquent message, but it got the point across." His arms tightened carefully around me. "I've been tracking you since you disappeared. Found your groceries scattered on the sidewalk. The butcher saw what happened."

"The dinner," I remembered suddenly, absurdly disappointed. "I was going to cook for you."

His smile was soft. "We'll have plenty of other dinners." His hand cupped my face with infinite tenderness. "Let's focus on getting you patched up first."

The sound of police and paramedics crashing through the underbrush grew louder. Voices called out, flashlight beams cutting through the darkness as they approached our position.

"Over here," Kronos called, not taking his eyes off me. His hand remained steady against my face, thumb gently brushing my cheekbone where it wasn't bruised.

"I need to tell you something," I said, the words coming out raspy through my damaged throat.

He shook his head. "Save your strength. We can talk after you're patched up."

"No," I insisted, gripping his shirt with what little strength I had left. "I need to say this now." I swallowed painfully. "I thought I was going to die out here, and all I could think about was never seeing you again. Never telling you…"

His eyes softened, the glow fading back to familiar silver. "Telling me what, love?"

"That I love you." I blurted out, afraid to hold back or I'd never get it out. "I love you, and I'm done running from this."

His smile was worth every ounce of pain I'd endured. "I know," he cooed, pressing his lips gently against my forehead. "I've always known."

The paramedics burst into the clearing then, equipment bags jangling, voices calling orders. Police officers secured Smokey, who was beginning to stir. Through it all, Kronos never let go of my hand, his eyes promising everything words couldn't say.

We had survived. Everything else could be figured out later.

www.ingramcontent.com/pod-product-compliance
Lightning Source LLC
Chambersburg PA
CBHW032302310726
48973CB00008B/2495